D0365673

# Here Goes Kitten

# Here Goes Kitten

*by*

Robert Gover

Grove Press, Inc. New York

Library of Congress Catalog Card Number: 64–13784
First Printing 1964



MANUFACTURED IN THE UNITED STATES OF AMERICA

# Here Goes Kitten

A lot of water has gone over the dam since I, James Cartwright Holland, last came upon the printed page, and therefore—for several reasons—I herewith return. The first of which is the remarkable literary success with which my first big opus, e.g., *One Hundred Dollar Misunderstanding*, met. Ergo, I am flattered to the quick by the undeserved praise my initial endeavor elicited from such renowned critics as, albeit for one, McCaffrey Dubinski, whose profound thesis, "Lack of Communication in the Modern World," has become a beacon in my life. And second, I am now a bona fide, certified writer—serious, professional, and committed—and therefore more capable of rising to the crying necessity to present this desperately needed sequel.

A desperation brought about not only by a second encounter with Kitten, but also, and especially, because of my political situation. Ergo, I find myself confronted by scandalmongers who are trying to dream up some way to somehow implicate me in what happened to another party—which I had absolutely nothing to do with. I was—yes—involved with that other party. Unfortunately, my involvement occurred shortly before his untimely death.

*Before* his death! I was not with him when he met his mysterious end, rest his soul. But, because of certain circumstances, some people around this Courthouse who *think* they are in the know, keep asking questions designed to cast suspicion in my direction.

Hence, whereas I launched my first narrative account as a college sophomore flunking three subjects—biology, psychology, and French—is it paradoxically ironic that, as of now, I am in danger of having my career scuttled, my reputation ruined, my means of achieving $15,000 take-home per annum—in short, that I am in danger of losing the fruits of all my efforts? Well, I am—that's precisely the danger I'm in.

Politics is the reason. More specifically, the pettiness of certain politicians, their narrow-mindedness as regards the public relations function in government, and their vindictiveness toward me because of the weight I carry around here.

Therefore, I must—with journalistic objectivity, detachment, and truth—give an account of exactly what took place that horrible weekend when Fate played a dominating role.

But let's take things step by step. Beginning with the fact that I've come successfully over the rocky road to academic fulfillment, a diploma, and am now J. C. Holland, B.S., out in the world on my own, where, thanks to my native ability for icy-clear analytical thought and salesmanship, I am employed by Hook County as Public Relations Director at $8,500 (before taxes) plus a $50-a-month expense account. (So, you see, I'm not rich, and, until I get some tax-free investments going for me, it'll be a struggle.)

One warm Friday afternoon in late August I was in my office with Betty Lu, my private secretary, and a gem of a girl, an indispensable addition to the County force, giving the taxpayer, as we all do, an hour's work for an hour's wages, and hers is not a position to be done away with, as certain misguided revisionists have advocated doing. Betty Lu, you see, was typing up a very key piece of literature—which I'll have more to say about later—when into my office walked none other than the illustrious Herman Pennypacker, Chairman of the Board of County Commissioners.

"Hello," said Herman.

"Hello," responded I.

Which no doubt seems like a simple exchange, on the surface of it, but in fact was fraught with ominous overtones, as I shall subsequently endeavor to reveal. For what Betty Lu was typing was a report I had just that day completed, a document destined to help stem the tide of welfarism in Hook County and reassert a cherished American ideal.

Well, after exchanging the above-mentioned misleadingly casual greeting, Herman sat down in a padded chair I keep stationed on the far side of my desk for visitors, and began contemplating. I say contemplating because he just sat there staring off into space, silently. Which is not the usual thing for our vigorous board head.

Pretending political naïveté, I said, "What can I do for you, Mr. Pennypacker?"

He cast me a meaningful glance but said nothing.

So let me take advantage of the illustrious Chairman's momentary silence to reveal my political commitments and fill you in on some significant details vis-à-vis the board head—his initial attitude toward old J. C. and the sterling victory he was now assured of. With the aid of my report!

When the position I hold first opened—at the creation of the board, just last June, to be precise—the board head had submitted to the board the suggestion that the Party District Chairman's son from his District be named to fill the post. However, State Senator Fitzwater Schlitzer, who not only put through the enabling act for the board's creation of the post, but, being from my town, a next-door neighbor in fact, realized I would graduate just as the post opened—the Senator let it be known that his selection was none other than J. C. Holland.

A selection which Mr. Pennypacker, rest his soul, took exception to, at first. Feeling, quite naturally, an obligation to his District Chairman.

He did, in fact, fight my appointment tooth and nail, until the Senator gave the green light go-ahead for the recent crack down on gambling and prostitution in the County's all-important Fifth District, which includes almost the entire City so has four or five times as many voters in it as the rest of the County combined. This crack down coming shortly before the last elections and having a beneficial effect: ergo, it shook the City administration to its boots and it unseated now ex-Commissioner Dodo Flipietro, who, as everyone locally knows unofficially, was intimately connected with nationally controlled Mafia-type racketeering interests in our City-County setup.

Hence, it ended as sort of a draw: Herman's choice from the Fifty, Seymour Herskovitz, to replace Flipietro, in exchange for me, the Senator's choice for the very sensitive Public Relations function, with the shake-up of that City gang thrown in as a bonus.

But it is not my purpose here to bore the lay reader with political nuances. The point which is really germane is that I'll readily admit, and have never denied, that Herman had not—until that Friday when he walked into my office—he had just simply never quite accepted me as a full-fledged member of the Party team, pulling my oar in the boat. He had—I'll make no bones about it—steadfastly ignored me.

And what brought him to my office this Friday was a controversy of vast significance: e.g., whether to shatter precedent, to cast to the winds tradition and principles as old as humanity, probably—or at least as old as Hook County—to shatter, as I said, by giving $3,000 of the taxpayers' hard-earned cash to buy food and fuel for so-called "unemployables"—whose race has nothing to do with it. A bunch of bums, virtually, an insignificant number, really, of people in the County with no resources, purportedly, and not qualified to be covered by any of the many existing welfare measures, such as Unemployment Compensation or Social Security, Old Age or Public Assistance, or even Relief. It was rumored—repeat, rumored—that some of this riffraff were *needy*. That was the rumor, and with winter approaching, none of them, reportedly, had heat, it was said, having unwisely exhausted the patience of fuel companies by far overstepping all reasonable bounds of credit.

Well, it's a shame that there *are* such people—true. And that they are right here in our political subdivision! I mean, I'm all for the elimination of poverty, *but!* In this land of freedom, diversity, and equal opportunity, should sacred tradition be thrown to the winds? Just to appease a pack of tramps, virtually, who won't work and plan ahead for their Golden Age? Who fail to educate their children properly and practically make a career out of taking advantage of the generosity of decent Americans?

Therefore—and in view of the fact that the newspaper publicity on these so-called unemployables had been simply horrible, having been engineered by those sob-sisters in Welfare—I had taken it upon myself to investigate their exact legal status and circumstances. I had not communicated my action directly to the Chairman, but I knew he would get wind of it sooner or later through unofficial channels. Because, you see, Mr. Pennypacker, as head of the majority faction, was leading the fight to defeat this much-publicized proposal.

And *that's* why our unprecedented hello's were fraught with such ominous overtones!

But, in all honest truth, I must say I was a bit bowled over to hear the Chairman break silence with the following:

"James, how about having dinner with me this evening at Blattenfeld's?"

And here, I must stress that it was *he* who invited *me*, not vice versa, as some have suggested. Nevertheless, it was an invitation I quickly accepted—though not so quickly as to appear anxious or insecure. An important aspect of politics, that appearance. I did, simply, give a straightforward nod, cheerfully.

Then, taking cognizance of all and sundry, I slyly interjected the following feeler concerning my report: "Anything you'd care to discuss at dinner, Mr. Pennypacker?"

"Oh," he chuckled good-naturedly, glancing at busy Betty Lu as she worked at my report in quadruplicate, "something may come up."

Following which, Betty Lu concluded her typing, precisely at 5 P.M., to be exact—threw me a wink to sustain me through what now loomed as a crucial ordeal, and left for the weekend. Herman, meanwhile, pounced upon my report and devoured it with ravenous eyes. And it was precisely at this juncture—while reading my report—that he took one of his customary heart pills. I want to broadcast that point and make it well known, for it's also been suggested that, due to his excitement over this or that other matter, the esteemed Chairman had neglected his medicine. Which simply just isn't so, for I saw him take that pill with my own eyes.

Well, anyhow, to make a long story short, we thereafter adjourned to Blattenfeld's, each driving his own car. I knew my report had impressed him: keen interest was evident on his massive countenance. In fact, even at this point I was so certain it had won his favor and welded our relationship, that I held to the possibility that he might feel me out on speech writing. Because, you see, he did plan to run for judge in the next election and, even though he was a brilliant politician, he wasn't what one might call literary. His forte was for politicking at the grassroots level; his genius, for holding the line against radical legislation. And even though he never got around to mentioning this, speech writing, I strongly suspect it was on his mind.

Because we did get well acquainted during that cordial dinner at Blattenfeld's. And if you care to check on that, I'm very sure there's a waiter or two there who was made aware of, and can describe, the cordiality we displayed. And I use the words *made aware of* advisedly: e.g., anyone who has ever heard the board head's voice knows how booming it is and how well it carries, and I'm no shrinking violet myself.

However, suffice it to say that our dinner was such a success that neither one of us cared to end the evening so soon. Thus, fortified by several double martinis, South African lobster-tail, etc., we thereafter drove—again separately—to a very interesting place of entertainment, in which we could be reasonably certain of two things: that we would see a good show, and that the Chairman's presence would not be conspicuous.

It's a nightclub called the Fish Pond, and it's a place old J.C. has been wont to frequent of late. And, even though it's rather famous hereabouts, as all advertisements for it justly proclaim, it's possible that you, Dear Reader, have never heard of it, for it's somewhat off the beaten path, and therefore I herewith render you the following sharply etched description:

Intimate—that's the key word. Dim lights, small round marble-topped cocktail tables with tiny blue lights on each, wrought-iron chairs with arms, and some of the most gorgeous waitresses one could find anywhere. In brief but tasteful attire. Then, swarming in a red inky ocean of neon above one, is this virtual sea of stuffed fish, dramatically illuminated and hung from walls and suspended from the ceiling. While over in one corner next to the stage is this big glass-enclosed water tank in which underwater ballets are performed.

You won't see anyone you know there—not in the lounge. Your own mother could be sitting at the table right next to yours and you'd never know it. It's that dark. The shaded blue lamp on each table is sufficient only to provide the immediate occupant with a general awareness of his drink. Thus, what looms prominent is the water tank near the stage and the sea of stuffed fish above. And the stage itself, of course, whenever an entertainer appears upon it and gets bathed in the spotlight.

So, after phoning ahead for reservations in the lounge (for otherwise one is relegated to the bar), off we went, Herman and I, political strangers no longer. Personal friends, in fact, and bound for whatever adventures might befall us in the enchantment of American nightlife.

Which is not to say that he neglected to take his heart pill after dinner, for I saw him take it. Maybe one of the waiters at Blattenfeld's will bear me out on that, too.

However, here we are in the lounge at the Fish Pond, watching a list of acts any Las Vegas club might easily envy, when lo and behold, who should appear upon that stage in front of that microphone with that spotlight full upon her, after having been introduced warmly by the master of ceremonies as Gigi Abercrombie, but a colored girl whose general appearance—in spite of a rather startling hairdo—immediately rang a bell. Faintly, at first. But then, when I heard her voice, the very first peep out of her, my mind focused and sharpened and cut into my memory like a knife!

It was Kitten! Yes, the very same girl I had met in that Negro whorehouse three years ago, and none other than the exact one my first literary endeavor was about.

Well! Needless to say, I was overwhelmed with surprise. How in the world did Kitten, of all people, end up a performing artist in the Fish Pond—a song stylist, so called. For as such was she introduced! That's what the master of ceremonies called her, sure as God made little green apples!

But in all honest truth, I should tell you right now that her style of singing was on about the same level as her . . . her style of earning a livelihood. Which is to say—well, to put it kindly, *earthy*. But to be a bit more accurate: low, vile, vulgar—i.e., an offense to the cultivated ear.

For her first selection, to cite just one example, she

mutilated "The Surrey with the Fringe on Top," from the renowned musical *Oklahoma.* Because certainly "Surrey" was not intended to be misconstrued the way this so-called Gigi Abercrombie (alias Kitten, alias God knows what all) misconstrued it. Surrey, as any dictionary will tell you, means: a pleasure vehicle having two seats, both facing front, and a horse. And if there aren't any legal restraints against the sort of defamation Kitten committed with that song, there should be.

Let me explain. Or try to, for although I am a writer—critically acclaimed as a literary artist, as well as of proven ability in the more practical field of public relations—I have never been called upon to serve professionally by describing such a manifestation as this colored girl's desecration of that great song. Which, as best I can present it, happened thusly:

*When I take you out in the surrey*
*When I take you out in the surrey with the fringe on top!*

Which are, of course, the actual true words of the song.

*However!*

And herein lies the point—every time she uttered the word *out*, she gently undulated her midsection forward, right in the face of the audience. And upon uttering the word *surrey*, she leered suggestively. So that by the time she got around to the *fringe on top*, it was evident to any close observer that she was *not* singing about a horse-drawn vehicle. On the contrary, she was, in fact, turning Oscar Hammerstein's great classic "Surrey" into an unsavory portion of the female anatomy.

Of this, I, for one, was certain. There could be no

doubt about it. Surrey, the way she twisted those fine lyrics, was not a horse-drawn vehicle, but a vehicle of another sort! Indeed, an object pertaining to no traffic whatsoever, save the illicit traffic of the flesh! What I mean to convey here is that she turned this perfectly innocent and mentally healthy song into something degrading, profane, sensual—downright cheap, in fact. (Or, instead of *cheap*, perhaps I should use the word *vulgar*.)

But, be that as it may, I need not overstress the fact, for the countless number familiar with my now-famous first effort, that, seeing Kitten on the stage at the Fish Pond as Gigi Abercrombie was a rather unsettling experience. For, you see, it was she, who, in the dastardly underhanded way of the underworld, pilfered over $100 from one James Cartwright Holland (that being my nom de plume) when he was a sophomore at good old State U., and she a common colored prostitute in one of those houses which, until our recent crackdown, flourished in this City.

I'll go so far as to tell you, in all honest truth, that it was virtually traumatic to encounter Kitten thusly. And so restraint—that's what was called for, and that's precisely the quality I did demonstrate. I was not about to let this traumatic encounter with Kitten disrupt the strong personal bonds of friendship and good fellowship being welded, that evening, with the board head.

What I'm trying to get across here is that, had I any intentions of ever again having relations with her—whether as Kitten or as Gigi Abercrombie—I could come back another night, by myself. And I certainly, at that time, had no intentions of raising the subject with the

Chairman. Even when, in my peripheral vision, I noticed that the expression on his face clearly revealed that he was . . . well, that he was quite taken by her . . . by her appearance.

Which surmise was substantiated moments later when she finished her second song—a matter I won't go into, having given you the general idea by the description of her first song. However, it is pertinent to mention that, following both these songs, the applause was *deafening!* Furthermore, Mr. Pennypacker, rest his soul, rose to his feet hooting with enthusiasm.

Here goes me, sittin at the bar with a couple johns, doin the spit-back, tryin t'make innerestin conversashun, an guess who come along? Guess who walk right up behind me an tap me on the shoulder?

Some trick I had in the cathouse three year ago. Yeah, some college boy I brung t'my partmin and we had this big thing with a hunner dollahs.

I mean it was a weekend, baby, an that's always a hunner, an this trick wasn't gonna pay up.

Anyhow, what I'm sayin, settin there tween these two johns an here come this thing outa my past. Tap, an I swing about on that stool, catch one look at that face—jes keep right on a-swingin till the stool's facin the bar again.

Like I never seen the mothah. Was only twirlin.

Cause soon's I lay eyes on that face, my belly goes tight on me. An it puts me t'scrambling up the stray pieces, tryin t'think what t'do, an he taps again.

Turn around slow this time, an here's this big ass of a white face hangin out on me like waitin for somebody t'push his button. All dress up like a man's magazine ad.

Is how he come on three year ago, too. Fashion plate. Big deal. Only difference, maybe he's a little bigger now.

Puttin that face on me like that, so I pertend I got a camera, hold it up t'my eye and I say, *Click!* Okay baby, got you pitcher.

An I swing back.

Then he grab ahold a me an turns me around, an he say, I sed Hello Kitten!

I say, Yeah baby, I heard what you sed, but you must have the wrong party, cause Mister, my name's Geegee.

Look real sad sayin this, like I'm awful sorry over his mistake.

Meet some ole trick out someplace an you don't know what t'do right off, this routine oughta turn him off, give you a chance t'think. Right?

I mean, baby, this one was more'n jes another trick. Was the very first weekend I ever had. An ooh-wee, did I ever fug up that weekend, too.

Anyhow, I try t'turn him off for a time, but he keeps right on a-comin, say, Hey Kitten, cut it out, don't act like you don't remember *me!*

Shake my head and make like I'm lookin him over real hard, tryin for all I'm worth t'remember, and like I jes *can't* for the *life* a me.

Then I turn my back on him—real slow this time, like you do on somebody's a little off his nut. Go back t'my drink, take a sip a whiskey an *pssst,* spit it back out inta the coke chaser.

That's the spit-back. Make them johns think you swillin down whiskey like mad. But you better not! Stuff they pour out for us entertainmin girls'll rot you quicker'n vee dee.

Anyhow, what I'm sayin, got my back on this thing outa my past, an I'm jes settin there facin front. Need time. Gotta figure out how t'be. These two johns I'm with gone pop-eye wonnerin what the hell it is with me, and this one behind me keeps comin on with this Kitten bit.

Me, I'm tryin t'come up with a way t'shake off everbody an gather up my sense. Took me too much by surprise, poppin up outa nowhere like this. So I need time. What I better do is, split and go way round the other side a the bar, make out with some johns over there, till I can think a some way t'handle this surprise.

Give the bartender a try, see if I can get him t'talk me out from unner this an let me take a breather, like I seen him do the other night for this other girl. Workin for this, got my eyes pinned on that bartender tryin t'meddle telepathy him the fug over here.

Leans over my shoulder an he say, Kitten you *must* remember me. My name's James Carright Hollan.

Oh yeah, baby, I remember okay. Tole me his name was

Jimmy three year ago. Yeah, an you know what else he tole me? Tole me he was a burgler, the dum she-it.

But I turn on him again an I say, Hell no I don't remember.

Comes back real quick with, Never mind that now, I'll refresh you memry later. Takes ahold a my arm an he say, Come on, I have a very distingwish gentlemin I wanna innerduce you to, a very great opportunidy if you play you cards right.

Here's me, I shake my arm loose, an I say, But baby! I ain't no cardplayer!

Then, here's the bartender, gonna find out what's goin on. Aks me, an I tell him this john think he *knows* me an I never *seen* the mothah. He got the wrong party, lookin for somebody name Kitten. Come on that bartender with my best most big-eye innosense bit, an I say, Can't be me, cause my name is Geegee. Right? Say, You know any Kitten workin here?

Cuts in an he say he don't care *what* my name is, *now*, he knows I'm the girl he lookin for, an he got this very distingwish party in the lounge he gonna innerduce me.

Then—you know what? That mothah goes an lays a fin on that bartender. Yeah, while he's jawin.

Does it real sly, but I catch it. Oh yeah, I catch that action, baby, I see that hand go sneakin over that bar an open on the other side an let somethin green fall. He don't sneak that past me, uh uh. I see that green go down behind that bar.

I ain't been here long, but I been here long enough t'know if you droppin gratooidies on these bartenders, it gotta be a fiver, cause they ain't gonna move for nothin less.

An this one—don't know his name, only been here a week, still ain't met everbody yet—this one *smells* that fin. Yeah, smells it like outa the corner a his eye, an he turns on me an he say, like he's talkin to a sick friend, he say, Admire of you talent in the lounge, Geegee. Why don't you go along with this gentlemin an meet him?

Well baby, what that means is, pick you black ass up an move it, girl.

Somebody gonna admire my talent in the lounge. In the lounge! Oh yeah, sure, okay, on my way.

Got no choice. Hop down an fall in behind followin.

That goddam bartender, he really pull a switcheroo, shippin my ass off like this. For nothin but a godam fin, too. An with this pee-petri-fuggin-fied burgler.

Don't know what I'm gettin into here, all I know is this ain't how it oughta happen. I mean, I had a feelin all along I'd meet up with this sumbitch again sometime, but not like this—walkin up behind me, scarin the daylights outa me.

If only I knowed that bartender, I coulda fix up a little *pause*, steada him pushin me off like this.

Gonna have t'make it with that bartender sometime, put him in my power. Yeah!

Cause I mean, baby, I got needs, got needs an requiremins, but takin off behind this mothahfuggah for a trip t'the lounge—that ain't one of 'em. Three year ago he come on in that cathouse fulla need an loaded down heavy with a wad a bills so big you could read the whole story clear through his clothes. An me, I went for it so hard

I dam near got driv back t'the cottinpatch fore we settled up.

Was when I first started husslin, didn't know my ass from a hole in the ground. Only went on what I got told. He'd a come on me like that a year later, baby, I'd a made his load light both ways slick as cuttin butter with a red-hot knife. But she-it, back then, I was only startin out.

Like now. Brand spankin new in this club, only jes tryin t'make my day-bue, my very first week here an this big importint first Friday night.

Well baby, you don't gotta be no fifty-cent palm reader t'get hip t'this scene. Right? I mean, this mothah's liable t'mess up my marbles all over again, I don't mind close what's goin on.

Guess the first thing I better do is, find out what's goin on inside that ofay skull, *this* trip, so I pull up alongside a him an slip an arm round his arm, an I say, Hey baby, who you say you's lookin for?

Look down on me hard, say, *You,* Kitten!

I don't even bat an eye. Say, Who this Kitten you keep sayin, baby? My name's Geegee.

*Horse*feathers! What he say, You's Kitten, an stop tryin t'pertend you ain't.

Gee-zuz! But I stay on it, say, But Lover, you got the wrong party! Ask anybody here, my name's Geegee. Cross my heart an hope t'die!

Laugh kinda shiddy, an then he comes on rattlin off real white. Lissen, he say, lissen, I'm willin t'let by-gones be by-gones, you jes put youseff in my hands an everthin'll be okay, gonna innerduce you t'this innerested party. . . . An he's off on that same ole noise again.

I cut him off, I say, *Really* baby, I don't go this crap, an I don't give a *clippedy clop* for you innerested party neither. An if I had me more *time* in this clipjoint, you'd sure have t'do more'n blow on the bartender t'pull this innerduce bizness in the lounge.

But that don't get me nowhere, jes pulls more yip-yappin outa him.

Comin on with this funny pitch, like he's got some kinda propazishun in mind, but I can't figure out—what he's sayin—jes what the hell it is. Up yakkin real high an mighty white for awhile, so I jes lean a-gin the wall, take up cleanin my nails an whistlin.

Then he comes down soft an smooth, an he say, Aw lissen Kitten, I need *help!* I need *you!* And I can make it worth you while, too—*if*, if you can get this gentlemin innerested in *you*. Do that, Kitten, an we all get what we want. Unnerstand?

No, but he's makin better sense now. Ain't pertendin he's a burgler, neither, this time. No, *this* time, he's comin on pimpin, like he's really pimpin.

That's the maybe of it, baby. That's how he's makin it seem.

But I ain't never been on one a these trips t'that motherin lounge before, an I ain't never heard nothin good about this kinda trip, so I keep right on shakin my head, say, No baby, uh uh, you draggin off the wrong party.

Ain't *draggin* me—is what he say—he's only a messinger bringin various parties t'gether for mewchal benefit.

Ah ha! He *was* a burgler, *now* he's a messinger. Humm.

Anyhow, yakkin away like this, we make it t'the curtin

they got separatin the bar an the lounge. Me, I'm still tryin for a way t'fug up this caper, if I can.

I mean, I don't mind bein part a no mewchal benefit thing, but this lounge bit—uh uh, no, I don't need that. So when I see who comes on carryin the flashlight, I make one more last try.

See, in the lounge, they got these coozie that carry lights, take you to a table. One comes for us is this one everbody say is Lizzy, so I give it a try.

Insurance, baby. I mean these lounge lizzards'll have you right under a table or somethin, but if you's makin it with this Lizzy, you got some help goin for you. Right?

Okay, now's my chance—last one fore he drags me inta the dark. So I give it a tumble—boy do I ever give it a tumble. Popeye wide at this curly blond coo, an I lick my lips real slow an sexy, roll a little hip an I jump one eyebrow up.

No go. All I get back is she runs them cold blue eyes over me, an I'm standin there with my tongue hangin out so far it's almost touchin the end a my nose, but it's no go.

Nex thing, here goes me, that sumbitch got me by the hand draggin me along, followin the light this Lizzy layin down, an we's goin deep right inta this mothahlumpin lounge.

Crazy place. Only time I ever really seen it was in the daytime when I first come here for audishun with Hap, an all it was then was jes a mess a tables an chairs, cigret butts all over the rug. But now, in the dark, this place's a livin breathin fishtank nightmare. Lit up fishes hangin all over lookin straight down on you like tryin t'neb in your bizness.

But *they* ain't what end up nebbin *my* bizness! No, cause here's me, I'm standin up a-gin this cold wall way over the far side—that Liz's split, an some big belly crowdin me back a-gin that wall, an they is hands goin ever which way, all over me, down my dress tuggin on my bra, an up my dress with a wigglin diddlefinger tryin t'poke a hole in my pants.

Gee-zuz! Like a flophouse fulla giant bedbugs, there for a minit. Pushin an pinchin an pokin everwhere. Kee-ryess! Movin my womanhood around like they think I'm a bushelbasket fulla tomatas.

Hands comin on me down from the top is the big one with the belly, an the ones goin up is the messinger, an they's boff tellin me tales I already know—from *way* back.

Then the messinger come out from scratchin around up my dress an he take ahold a my hand, an *then* what he done is, he *push* my hand at this big belly's bizness! Tryin t'make it seem like *I'm* doin this—like *I'm* reachin for this innerested party's privates! Yeah!

Kee-ryess!

An he woulda made it with this hussle, too, if my hand'd hit the handle. But she-it, far's I know, this innerested party's all belly, no bizness.

Well anyhow, what I'm sayin, I don't fight this. Too dark. Ain't about t'get myself in trouble way back here, get put down right on the floor, an nobody ever know it. Less they come walkin along an stumble over me in the dark.

No, all I do is, I jes stay pinned there with all this grabbin goin on tryin t'fug up my dignidy, an I hear the jelly belly jabberin off at me on somethin, can't hear what.

Rumble rumble. But like it ain't comin through. We's titty t'belly an his head's so far up over me I can't even see it, hardly, an I sure ain't hearin a word he sayin.

Then the big one moves away, pulls his paw outa my dress an moves offa me like all this grabbin never happen. An the messinger takes ahold a my hand again—he sure do wanna hold hands—an this time he stuff somethin crumbly in it.

I know right off it's green. Can tell by the feel. Oh yeah!

I say, Propazishun?

Shhh!, he say, watch what you say! See ya later, backstage.

Me, I still don't know what the fug's going on, really, an that goddam messinger got a point about not talkin—not back here near the wall. In this club, baby, the walls got ears! Yeah. Bugged, this Fish Pond.

So I la-dee-dah back the hell outa here, hangin on tight t'that crumble in my hand.

An gettin out ain't real easy, neither. Don't got that Liz with the light, gotta make it on my own. End up bumpin on knees an steppin on toes, crackin my hip on some hard-ass chair, an gettin my butt pinched—Kee-ryess! They sure name this club right—Fish Pond. Fore I'm haff way out, I'm sure this place's jes swarmin with fish, an ever one tryin t'take a little nibble outa me. Can hardly make it outa there without gettin chewed t'pieces.

But I finally get through that curtin. Get out a there, an take a deep breath. Don't look t'go back in real soon. That goddam bartender can jes find hiseff some new way t'make a five. Yeah!

Gee-zuz, way the man tole me, us entertainmin girls

spose t'work the johns in the bar. Oh yeah, the big money's in the lounge, you can't get them bar johns t'turn loose any really signifigant gratooidies, hardly, cause if they had it, they'd be in the lounge too. Other hand, I never hear any girl say she rung up no good big jingle by goin inta the lounge in the dark!

One coo name Wanda, been here over a year now, she tellin me, she say this Friday night crowd's the roughest any place. But me, straight outa the black an blue, five dollahs a throw, I figure that chick don't know what *rough's* all about.

Hey, you wanna know somethin? She does. Oh yeah!

Gettin outa the lounge ain't the end a my thing with these nibblin fish, neither. No, cause direckly I'm in through the curtin, here comes this big gang a johns, jes a-pourin in that front door like they's no end to 'em.

Blockin my way, so I gotta plow through. Big mob scene. Land in the middle a this jam, an pretty soon I feel fingers wrap around my butt an squeeze—squeeze baby, like he gonna take the left cheek with him when he goes.

Like, *too much!*

So I lay an elbow on him, hard. Musta found me the right spot, too, cause I hear *Offf!* An that's the end a that, I'm loose an on my way again. Musta got him right below the ribs, but I don't turn around t'check, jes keep on a-goin like it never happen.

Due on pretty soon. Don't stop t'jaw no more johns. Go straight back t'the dressin room an take a quick look at this balled up bill, see what kinda money this mothah layin down for his pussy these days.

There may be a fairytale-maker or two in this County who might try to suggest that Mr. Pennypacker's involvement with Kitten—covered later in this account—came about at *my* instigation. But as you'll see, Dear Reader, this is not true. So pay no attention to any such suggestions, should they be forthcoming. From no matter what source. Assuming you are the mature, aware, Hip person you must be to read this account, you surely must know very well that everyone has enemies who constantly assault one with the most flagrant rumor-mongering. And in politics, it's even worse!

So, let me tell you, with true journalistic detachment, exactly what happened. Which was this:

As Kitten retired from the stage after executing her slaughter of those two songs she sang in the first of several appearances, Mr. Chairman—to my utter surprise and complete chagrin—said, applauding for her furiously as he spoke, "Charming girl! Amazing talent! Boy, those Negroes certainly do have rhythm, don't they."

"Yes, they certainly do," said I.

I'm not usually such a conformist, but I saw no reason to dampen the board head's enthusiasm at that time. He was having such a ball I just went along with it. I applauded, and loudly. No matter how deeply shocked I was inside my own private heart, no matter how greatly surprised by his reaction to her performance, no matter how captivated by her—if you'll pardon the expression—charms.

For he had been captivated. That was plainly evident. Long after she'd left the stage, he kept talking about her. In fact—not to be disrespectful or anything—but he kept up this enthusiastic chatter, exclaiming how he had never seen such a—well, such a *sexy* colored singer. I made several pointed attempts to direct his attention to the other performers, especially to the Egyptian belly dancer, who is also non-white but not at all uncultured, and with a most delightful milk-chocolate hue, and who is, I should add, an acquaintance of mine from other sojourns to the Fish Pond. But he'd have none of it; he definitely was strongly attracted to Kitten. Gigi. I went so far as to explain what a strongly erotic individual this exotic dancer is—having ascertained this personally on several prior occasions—but nothing would deter him from his glowing interest in Gigi.

Not that I was trying to arrange some sort of double date type affair where I'd go with Kitten and he with the belly dancer. No such thing; my one and only interest was to honor his standing by doing what I could to enhance the pleasure of this fine evening, especially since he had been working much too hard recently and was in acute need of diversion.

Believe me, I did my level best to ignore his enthusiastic exclamations as long as I could. Albeit, I tried desperately to direct his attention to the other entertainers, as mentioned. I even went so far as to blatantly tell him that colored singers like this (alias) Gigi Abercrombie were a dime a dozen, but he simply would not listen. Ergo, he finally became so insistent, so interested, so fascinated by this . . . this song stylist, that I at last found myself on the horns of a most thorny dilemma:

Should you, J.C., I asked myself, inform him (Herman) that the object of his excessively keen admiration is an old, however fleeting, friend of mine? (Well, no, not *friend. Chance acquaintance* is the word we want here.) Not that I harbor hostile feelings about the money she stole from me. No, because it taught me a valuable lesson, a lifelong lesson. For that experience did, I assure you, improve my Lifesmanship considerably. By making me see with icy clarity that one must follow in the path taken by one's elders and betters, for therein lies the true road to adult maturity.

And if—to return to my self-interrogation—if I do tell him of my acquaintance with her—what then? Should I shatter his illusion (*sic*, understandable from certain angles) by revealing her *real* identity?

Not that one could be entirely unsympathetic to Mr. P.'s appreciation of her appearance, taken objectively all in all, and putting aside for the moment the mangling she gave whatever song she chose to sing. She had filled out in the past three years, especially in the bust, and the gown she wore seemed expressly to show one that she wore no brassiere, and that she had . . . well, I'll put this rather bluntly; there's no reason to beat around the bush—that she had large, protruding boobs. In addition to which her hips and derrière seemed to have taken on even more arresting curves and contours.

Not that I was at all attracted to her myself, or even moved. What I'm trying to point out here is that, seen objectively, she did present an attractive appearance. In a very gaudy and cheap sort of way, and providing you are without racial prejudice. So that Mr. Pennypacker's fascination is not at all impossible to understand.

Hence, in the end, I finally decided that, in view of our party affiliation, and especially because we were now at last becoming truly political teammates in spite of our original differences, I finally decided to tell him. Whereupon, I said:

"Herman, I think I know that colored girl."

That, in effect, is what I said, and his amazed surprise was evident when he responded: "*What?*"

"Yes," I said, "the Negress singer."

"You know her?" blubbered the board head.

(Well, no, not *blubbered*. Let's change that to *blurted*.)

"You think you know her," blurted the Chairman.

"Yes," I said. "In fact," I continued, now cognizant of Mr. Pennypacker's mounting interest, "I'm sure I do. Met her at State U."

And before I could revise that slightly misleading phrasing of my relationship with Kitten, the board head had bounded like a spirited foxhound to the conclusion that Kitten had been a colored co-ed at State U. An erroneous assumption to the *nth* degree, as any reader of my critically acclaimed first narrative will readily attest.

Forthwith, Herman said, "Well well well. Why didn't you say so in the first place, James?" And he then went on to say, "I suggest that we seek her out, escort her here, and have a few words with her."

You see, Dear Reader, it was, as I've repeatedly told everyone, really *his* idea, not *mine*. I was merely acting on his behalf. My only personal temptation being that I couldn't help wondering how she would respond to the sight of none other than James Cartwright Holland when, there before her I'd stand, victim of a somewhat perverse and senseless misdemeanor perpetrated three years ago by none other than herself. A misdemeanor which I was inclined to suspect had been festering in her puss-bag of a conscience ever since. Assuming she eventually achieved realism enough to acquire a conscience, that is. Would she run? Would she faint? Would she offer to repay the money? Or would she simply pretend not to recognize me?

The board head then went on to explain what he planned to do when he met her—why, that is, he wanted to meet her. But, in keeping with the sacred traditions of literature, I shall leave these plans of his in abeyance. At least for the time being. Suffice it to say only that I acted on his behalf, at his suggestion, when I made my way out of the lounge and into the bar, where I spotted her immediately, her dark color making her more than a little conspicuous—perched on a stool at the other end of the bar, sitting between two youths who looked like a couple of rubes, plying them with drinks.

Well, I walked up to her, tapped her on the shoulder and presented myself. She turned around and, in spite of an obvious attempt to pretend she didn't recognize me, she flinched.

Having correctly anticipated that she might pretend not to recognize me, I was not put off by her tactics—namely, by her attempt, doomed from the very beginning, to act like she didn't. Largely for the benefit of those two country bumpkins she was with, I surmised, because it was evident that they didn't know how to handle these B-girls.

But, with the help of Paul, the bartender, an old friend of mine from other evenings on these stools, I managed to defeat her ruse, get the situation in hand, and soon was escorting her out of the bar, back into the lounge, toward an introduction with Herman.

An introduction which resulted in Mr. Pennypacker's giving her a small token of his appreciation—for her, shall we say, *effort* as an entertainer. As well as for his admiration of her as a member of a minority group making good in our Free Society.

I, of course, did not share this esteem, nor the special quality of his admiration, having behind my fewer years enough experience with this so-called Gigi Abercrombie to make a more realistic assessment of her present situation. And I certainly had no intentions of touching her, none whatsoever, at this time, because after all, she was, and still is, a harlot of criminal inclinations, now hiding behind a new alias, but the same colored prostitute nevertheless.

However, before I proceed any further, I should add that I had, indeed, *warned* the board head. Never let it be said that I introduced him to her without fair warning!

Following which, bringing them together was interesting—watching Kitten peer up over the distinguished Mr. P.'s brawny expanse, trying to see his face and catch what he was saying. While the Chairman stood there with a kindly hand on her affectionately, the two of them slightly uncertain, both trying to make conversation, as I hovered close by attempting to aid their efforts to communicate.

And, at this point, I might stray off course a bit, just enough to demonstrate for you what a terribly amusing thing that conversation was, for they became, right there and then, two living symbols of McCaffery Dubinski's thesis, lack of communications in the modern world today. Kitten, being rather diminutive, you see, was not tall enough, even in those spiked heels she wore, to be on the same level with the kingsized Herman, who did not choose to bend down condescendingly to her. So they were conversing on different levels, literally! I was able to hear them both, being considerably taller than Kitten but shorter than the eminent board head, and what they said was, quite precisely, this:

The Chairman asked her how she liked the entertainment business; Kitten said, "What?" The board head asked her what she did in her spare time; Kitten said, "What?" Mr. Pennypacker told her he enjoyed her performance; Kitten said, "What?" Herman said he'd very much like to meet her later informally and asked her to accept the abovementioned small token of his appreciation; Kitten said, "What?"

Following which, Kitten returned to her B-girl duties at the bar and the Chairman and I continued to develop our increasingly congenial friendship by a jovial tête-à-tête concerning his abortive, however comical, encounter with the newest of the Fish Pond's attractions.

Shiverin shitfits!

Know how much that cheap messinger slip me? One pissy-ant fin! Yeah, one bartender-size five! Jes one two three four five-oh!

Baby, that five won't even cover damage to the dress! Oh yeah, it's the club's dress an all, but I *mean!* The sumbitch wanna slip me somethin, he oughta come on with somethin signifigant. Like at least twenty.

That motherin messinger must think he still a burgler back in the cathouse, gonna get what he lookin for by layin down five.

Hey, I got news for him! One thing he gonna have t'learn *real* quick—they's been some changes made. Yeah!

Jes wait'll I see him again. Gonna wad this bill up in a spitball an shoot him right in the eye, tell him t'messinger *that* propazishun!

But right now I gotta come off all that. Put that five in my pocketbook and go t'pattin down my hair an straightenin my dress up, fixin t'go on.

Then, surprise surprise!

Guess who pop right in. Yeah, walk in that door like he owns the club. Stand there a minit and we give each other a good hard lookin over in the bright light.

Then I grab my purse an pull out that five, an I straighten it out longwise, an I hold it up over my head an wave it at him, say—jes like the disarmin little dolly I am —I say, I *do* believe you *drop* this by mis*take*, Lover. You shouldn't be so *care*less with you money.

He stands there, don't make a move. So I say, Oh! It ain't yours?

An he say, What's the matter, Kitten? Not enough?

She-it. By this time, my arm's tired so I take it down an I say, Enough? Enough for what?

Starts tellin me how it was jes for openers, like t'get me innerested, an he's blowin off like that. Me, I cut him off that bullshid, I say, Man you think you gonna raise any innerest with this kinda figure . . . Baby, you better back up some an come at that mewchal benefit thing one more time. Yeah, once again!

An before he had a chance t'say boo t'that, I quick hit him with this—I say, Nother thing, didn't I see you slippin that bartender a five?

Catch him flatfooted with that. Stands there with his mouth hangin open a minit, then he say, Sure he gave the bartender five.

Okay, that's the goin rate—for bartenders! But you musta been outa you mind when you put a fin in *my* hand.

Says he don't unnerstand.

Course you don't, baby. Tell you another thing—I don't unnerstand neither. But that's the game, Lover, an that's why you all fugged up. An that's why I'm givin you back this bill. Like let's jes say you drop it by mistake, okay?

But he come back with no no no, was no mistake, put that money in my hand, wants me t'have it. Rattlin off like that till I cut him down with this—I say, But Lover! I ain't innerested!

An I toss that bill on the floor right by his feet, say, Now take it an leave. Beat it, flake, fug off, vamoose, split, get the everlovin hell outa here an let me get ready t'go on!

Turn my back on him and go right on fixin up like he ain't even here.

Nobody says nothin for a time. Room's fulla breathin. Then he say—in this low voice like maybe he done gave up tryin t'put me on—he say, Not enough, eh.

An I figure I'm off to a pretty good start in this club. I mean, you get a rep for goin cheap, baby, an you had it.

So I don't say a word back, jes keep on with my hair.

Okay, he say, how about fifty?

I quick tell him t'hush up, don't say them numbers out loud.

Got one in here too, eh. What he say.

I say, *Hush!* Make a motion for him t'come on over, an I get down on my knees an show him the bug they got in this dressin room—unnerneath the table, stuck up there on the bottom a this dressin table like a dead cockaroach. Gets down by the side a me an takes a look.

An before he gets back up, guess what. Lays down a fifty. Yeah, right there by my knees.

I stand up by that fifty. Never grab nothin right off, always wait a minit, hold it, act like you thinking it over.

Then he comes up close t'my ear an whispers, says this jes a *down*paymin, says he got *cart*blanch, is what he say, cartblanch an him an the bored head gonna see I's well paid for the pleasure a my company. Another fifty at least, an maybe more!

Hummm.

Pulls back offa me an he say a little louder, he say, They's gonna be a party later on after the club close, an this party gonna be in some motel, an you's invited.

I say, *What* motel.

Say, Never mind *what* motel. Gonna decide that later. First things first. Can I make this party?

Ummm, I guess so.

Comes up close again an he says in my ear, Hey Kitten, I'll tell you a little secret—this man's high up in politics, so if you make him like you, you got it made! Then he winks real sly an he say, Sides that, me an you can get re-acquainded.

Well baby, the time has *def*nitly come for me t'quit himmin and hawin around. I mean, he's right—you make it with some big politicko an you got a good thing goin. So! Time for me t'reack!

I turn on this nice warm smile an plant a little kiss on his cheek.

Smiles back, pats my black ass, tells me he'll see me later, an then he cuts out the door.

But right now, baby, I don't got time t'even think about it. Gotta hop an go. Due on any minit now. An maybe I'm late. Zoom outa here an get behind that curtin.

Don't get there none too soon, too. Bump right inta this stripper comin off, dam near get run down. I mean, this stripper, she's a great big thing with legs on her the size a my hips, dam near. Out weigh me three t'one, I bet. Hate t'tangle with *her*. An she's another one ain't exactly friendly with me, too.

Anyhow, what I'm sayin, I'm on. Scare me ever time I go out on this stage. An t'night I took five pees already, feel like I gotta go again. But they ain't no chance for that. The man's out there talkin on the mike, givin this big line on me, sayin how I'm a new talent discovry.

Nex, here goes me, out there in the bright lights. An when I say bright, I *mean* bright. Really, baby, all you can see when you out here is them hung-up, lit-up fishes. You can't see no parts a that audience.

Well, you *can* see a little bit a the bar. But I mean you sure go blind t'the big money in the lounge.

What I do, t'get off bein scared, is I talk t'them fishes. Hey! What I'm sayin, I talk t'them fishes in my head. I mean I make believe I'm talkin.

Seem like the color a my skin give me a thing with them fishes. We both got that high visibility—right? An we's both sorta hung-up, too.

So t'night, this big first Friday night I gotta make it, cause this my first week here an that's call a day-bue an if

I make it, the man say he gonna put me on steady, forty a week plus tips, gratooidies an favors.

Well baby, I *know* that forty won't go nowhere, but tips, gratooidies an favors—hey-hey, that's a whole new world!

Anyhow, what I'm sayin, t'night I'm like talking t'them fishes in my head, I'm sayin, Hey fishes, don't you ever get scared, hangin up there over them invisible ofay? You ever get haff's scared's me?

Takes my mind off it, talkin like that.

Then the group's inta my number—You call it madness but I call it love—an I'm gettin set t'sing. I never sung with a group till last Monday night. Gee-zuz, I never even sung, period. I mean, you know, in front of an audience an all. But we gettin better an better, me an the group. Last Monday we was like on diffrent songs, dam near. But t'night we's makin it okay, knock on wood.

So then I crack inta this madness song an I put it over, too. Then I sing my other number—Got you unner my skin.

Can put more inta this one. It's a good song t'sing t'them invisibles, too, cause it's true. Oh yeah, all kinda ways.

I mean, *they* don't dig it *no* way, I spose, but I *sing* it *my* way.

Some entertainmin girls around here worry what t'do with they hands when they's singin. She-it, not me. I don't *do* my hands. I let 'em do jes whatever the song makes 'em *feel* like doin. Yeah!

An this skin song give me a chance t'shake a little ass, too. Like do a little shimmyin cha cha. Sooner or later, baby, that shakin gonna pay off, fetch me out some big money from that motherin lounge.

I mean, I ain't for goin in there, like I had t'do t'night, but if he comes out after me, I won't turn it down.

Anyhow, them invisibles down there go for it, cause when I'm done that second number, they turn loose with more clappin—pretty near loud's my first number t'night.

Flips me, that clappin. Whistlin too. Makes the back a my neck tickle.

Course, I know you can't allow that clappin t'be the end. Jes gotta take it an forget it, go right on practicin you style an don't let all that crap get ya.

So I go off bowin an bendin, bobbin an backin up, smilin up so wide I'm showin every tooth in my head.

Then—soon's you off, you gotta go back out t'the bar an set t'work all over again, jawin the johns.

I turned at this juncture to an interrogation of the Chairman's specific plans, for he had hitherto only sketchily outlined them. And since they are an integral part of this account, I have decided that I can—with confidence and while staying within my legal rights as a literary artist—divulge them to you, Dear Reader, without impairing in the slightest the high standards I've set, even though they may seem shocking to some.

But I feel I must interject, right here, a warning: namely, that it is not my intention to slander the good name of the late Mr. Pennypacker, rest his soul. And if these events tend to become a mite sordid—that is to say, if the board head's behavior seems a bit . . . shall we say, *earthy*—please understand that, by giving the actual details of what transpired, I am not slandering his memory, but merely proclaiming the truth to set the record straight.

Besides which, Mr. Pennypacker was not an effete, by any means. He was a full-bodied man of flesh and blood appetites, and even in his sixties and despite his heart condition, he was not one of your nice-nellie types, and if you take the trouble to ask those who knew him in his youth, I'm sure you'll learn that, with the ladies, he could always hold his own.

Ergo, what Herman had in mind was this: he planned to reserve by telephone a large family suite at a nearby motel, where the three of us could assemble. It was his intention to buy sex from Kitten. I was to be on hand to see that she held up her end—that she didn't try to rob us, or something.

Meanwhile, I was to handle the agreement with her, and with the Chairman's carte blanche as to whatever fiscal demands she might make, was to escort her to the rendezvous, a motel about half an hour's drive from here. (And, as usual, I refuse to serve prurient interests by naming that establishment.)

Well, I assured him I'd be glad to do all this—as a favor to him, for I had no desire to have relations with the girl myself. Then, just as I was about to depart for a little conference with her on the subject, the board head added a surprising bit of information—in the form of a warning.

"Be careful what you say, James," he said, "for this nightclub is bugged."

"Bugged!" I exclaimed. "Are you sure?"

"Yes," he said, "I am sure."

"But why?" I implored. "I mean, I don't want to seem naïve, but such a thing does sound like it may be an invasion of individual privacy, it would seem. On the surface of it."

"No," he assured me, "in this case, it's merely a legal tool of local government. This club, you see, was a favorite hangout for the old Flipietro gang, and even though they're out of power now, this place is still under surveillance."

Well, this was a nuance I was thankful to know, and could well understand the logic, legality, and morality behind the bugging of the club, for such political cancers are not easy to stop, once they're started. However, there was no time for pondering the interesting pieces of the political puzzle, for I was on my way backstage, on behalf of the board head, to discuss stipulations with Kitten.

A discussion which turned out to be not such a simple thing. Albeit, no sooner had I come upon her—in this moldy, broken-down dustbin they call a dressingroom—than she launched a series of impertinent responses. That is to say, no sooner had I walked into this dressing room to find her sitting on a wooden chair with the back broken off it, in front of this mirror which has endured such a series of shatterings that it is now more a study in fragmented vision than a reflection of any who might gaze into it—no sooner had I come upon her thus than she took from her handbag the Chairman's present, a $5 bill, and thrust it up at me indignantly. She did, in fact, intend to give it back—to refuse it! Moreover, she had the unmitigated gall to imply that Mr. Pennypacker is not the generous, big-hearted man he is (I mean, *was!*).

For a moment, I was tempted to shed civilized restraint and let her know in no uncertain words just how lucky she was to even be noticed by our County's leading luminary. Discretion, however, won this battle with my rage, and I controlled myself enough to appeal to the abject smallness of her greedy little sub-mind, to broach the matter of the moment by assuring her that her petty demands for more money were, because of the subject's standing in the community, entirely a matter of secondary importance —and that I had a carte blanche to negotiate with her. In effect, I let her know that when the board head seeks his pleasure, price is no obstacle. It is, I further told her, hardly a matter to be even discussed!

This much cleared from the charred rubble of our relationship, I approached her on the subject of price. (I realize this business is a distasteful passage for the cultivated reader, but please bear with me, for it is one of the sinuous muscles which binds my account together.) Ergo, she replied to this by asking the exorbitant, however significant, sum of $100.

Well! I gulped my astonishment, shuddered at the implications, and calmly ignored her much-too-overt attempt to add insult to injury, the financial as well as emotional injury she caused me three years ago when $100 loomed prominent. Your task, J.C., I now told myself, is not to become involved with this Negress personally. That, thank goodness, is behind you now. Your task now is to pave the way for Mr. Pennypacker, to act as his agent, his emissary, and above all to keep personal feelings out of it.

Hence, overriding this trollop's reckless nervyness, I responded in a way I'm sure she thought I wouldn't—namely, by reaching into my pocket and making her, right there and then, a cash advance of $50. Following which I informed her that the other $50 would be paid upon her upholding her end of our agreement.

And that was that. Except that, just for a moment, things did look bleak—i.e., she became guarded, as if she regretted naming such a significant sum. But this guardedness was but a moment of turning, I quickly saw, for until then she had steadfastly denied remembering me. Now it became clearly evident that the very sight of me was indeed as salt in the wound of her gashed and bleeding conscience.

Which is not to say that the quote conscience unquote of a colored prostitute is the same as the average woman's. That is, I'm keenly aware that Kitten's morals are so low as to be practically infinitesimal.

But I was afraid that if I didn't tickle the palm of her clutching hand with a sum larger than the esteemed board head's deposit, she would demand some completely unacceptable figure, something so far-fetched in its exorbitance that we couldn't possibly meet it.

Thus, the $50. Which I was reasonably certain Mr. Pennypacker wouldn't miss, even though at the time the actual currency came from *my* pocket. (Although, as Fate would have it, he never did, the way things turned out, have an opportunity to reimburse me. But that's an unimportant detail, comparatively.)

To continue: this out of the way, I returned to the Chairman with the cheery news that the deal had been consummated. I thought it best, at that time, to withhold the details; later, I reasoned, his mind would be more receptive to entertaining and appreciating certain overtones implicit in that price.

As for now, the next step was the reservation of the motel room, a step I forthwith took in a telephone booth in the club's main lobby, enjoying a distinct advantage in this matter because the owner of this particular motel is an old frat brother of mine, and—with several past dealings under my belt—I'm well acquainted there, even with the desk clerks, so was able to stipulate precisely what room I wanted—in this case an entire family suite, as mentioned.

The matter of the reservations out of the way, Mr. Pennypacker said that since he could use a little rest, having had a rather trying day, he would leave immediately for the motel, where reservations had been made—under an assumed name, of course!—take a little catnap, and be waiting for me when I arrived later with Kitten.

So I bade him good-bye and saw him to the door, and I thereafter transferred my drink from the lounge to the bar, stopping by Kitten just long enough to tell her everything was set. She was still milking those two youths, incidentally.

I remained at the bar, leaving my drink only once—to go backstage and settle some details of the final arrangements. These made—after a series of off-color activities and remarks I won't bore you with—I spent the rest of the time until her 3 A.M. quitting hour talking to others at the bar.

Kitten, during the course of her B-girl activities, didn't deem to stop by and talk with me, which was just as well. I have a rather solid reputation at that establishment which her patronage would not have enhanced.

Certainly she wasn't the sort one would expect to encounter at the Fish Pond. She was, because of her race, causing quite a stir. One might even go so far as to say that she was, in fact, a dark apparition—a wild defiance of the statistics of sociological probability, having somehow managed such an incomprehensible jump as graduating from a cheap brothel to a posh nightclub. Nevertheless, here she indeed was, guzzling drink after drink of top-shelf whiskey. With a coke chaser, of all things! Surely a sickening combination for the cultivated imbiber to contemplate, whiskey and coke chaser.

Now without getting involved in racial matters or semantics, I should, just to fill you in, add that one couldn't help noticing how large a role in her B-girl activities her color played. Ergo, imagine yourself at the bar of the Fish Pond—suddenly confronted by this Negroid face, maybe peeping around your arm as you sit at the bar, and you turn and there are these gleaming teeth and eyewhites coming at you out of the semi-dark atmosphere, and above that this mop of jet black hair in this radical upsweep or beehive, whatever it's called. Indeed, her appearance at that bar was almost as shocking as her . . . her style of singing, and more than one customer did a double-take, I noticed.

And . . . well, thus the time passed, uneventfully, until 3 A.M., when I drove her to her date with the Chairman.

Fifty dollahs is fifty dollahs—right? Okay, an like Hap say, Take the money an run.

Same time, I better watch where I'm runnin, goin off with this mothah give me such a hard time three year ago.

Cause baby, that was a bad scene. A sad action, an if it hadn't been for this girlfriend name Jackie, that burgler'd took me. Was only startin out then, workin that cathouse. Never made nothin on the side before.

Took advantage, what he done. Come on wavin that big wad at me an then he tried t'run off without payin up. An *then,* he took this ole lady's car! The madam run the place I was in.

Anyhow, what I'm sayin, everbody dependin on this new gig I got t'bring home the bacon, but recallin what happen with this burgler-messinger that other time, I'm all for goin slow on this propazishun he's puttin out t'night.

Wish I had me more *time* in this club. I mean I'm pretty sure I got this gig knocked up, now, but the man still ain't sed boo.

But she-it, I had the house brung down right from my very first number t'night! Had them invisibles beatin they hands somethin awful!

So I don't think he gonna let me go. No, an like startin nex week I can really operate, an if this messinger'd a come on then—

Is the really main fugup. I mean, why ole lady luck put him on me t'night. . . . More'n I even wanna *think* about!

He's beginnin t'look like a *thing* in my *life!*

But somethin come you way like this, it don't do no good t'try t'duck it, does it?

Okay then, grossery money for the I double A double P. Name a this place I'm livin at. Stand for Internashunal Associashun for the Advancemin of Po*lite* People.

Yeah I know that's a cornball name, but I can't help it, that's what we call it. Way out in the country, some ole house, nobody there but us chickens.

Got one big advantage—no rent. Jes a place everbody forgot was there, an if somebody own it, he ain't sayin.

I mean, it ain't the Hotel Aster, but I ain't Queen 'lizabeth neither.

Anyhow, everbody countin on this gig a mine for grosseries. So low on cash right now we's about ready t'come on the nex cashier with stones.

That's the sum cottinpickin total, an that's the monkey on my back with this pimpin propazishun. Gee-zuz, baby, I ain't got no choice!

Anyhow, I'm back with them same two johns, the young ones, order up my see an double you, an I'm carryin on the spit-back an the innerestin conversashun bit.

Ain't up settin there a minit, when—whoops! Here he goes, again. Catch a sight a him outa the side a my eye, struttin right through this Friday night bar crowd like he's smokin the best. Right up t'my left shoulder an tap, again, an this time he whisper in my ear —real windy, like sexy—say, Other party gone t'the motel, Kitten, everthin's set.

Then he moves on around the end a the bar and goes t'the other side, find hiseff a stool over there. Orders up somethin in a short glass an jes set there, swishin the ice cubes an watchin me—with this *def*nitly shiteatin grin!

Me, I'm wound up with these two johns, got my hands full keepin them alive.

Got a bad hang-up with this innerestin conversashun thing, an the man first tole me that's what I'm gonna do, I *swear* I didn't have th*e fog*giest.

But I must be doin better now. Had four nights practice, an with these two I got some kinda innerestin somethin goin, cause both these jackrabbits peekin down my dress like they think a dinnerbell gonna ring any minit.

Bartender keeps comin over, leanin on his elbow near me. She-it. I know what he wants. Wants me t'tell him how I made out in the lounge, but I jes leave him hangin. Looks at me an then he looks over at that messinger, an then he looks back at me.

Piss on that bartender. Gonna stay right where I'm at. Gonna put off circilatin long's I can. Gonna cool that messinger till I'm dam good an ready.

Useta daydream I'd meet him again sometime, an I useta know, in my daydream, jes how I'd act. Yeah, he'd wanna make it up t'me counta bein such a fuggin fink like he was, so he'd pick me up, fix me up with some nice clothes an a place t'live an all, an we'd get a good thing goin. Yeah, an then I'd jes give him the best godam lovin he could ever hope t'get.

But I never daydream the sumbitch'd come poppin up in no mothahfuggin nightclub, surprise me outa my wits. Yeah, an on top a that, lay down some pimpin jelly-belly propazishun!

Settin over there with that grin on his pussysugger an them love-sick eyes jes a-lickin all over my face—ever-time I look over he's starin right back, an when I ain't lookin I can feel them eyes warmin my cheek.

An what I don't go, baby, is, if he so warm for my form why don't he jes *say* so. Me an him could take off someplace an have it out. I mean what's all this he's pullin with the innerested party? That fat one *own* him or somethin?

Could take care a that politicko *too*. Some *other* time.

Hey, workin the cathouse or the Paradize Hotel ain't no snap, baby, but at least you don't run inta none a this trickydicky stuff, some trick outa you past playin two ends a-gin the middle.

Is the only way I can figure it, what he's up to.

So! What I do, I stay put with them two till Sharmain goes on—she's the other color girl workin here, 'gyptian belly dancer come from Alabama, talks real uppity. Stripper follows her, an then me. So right here, I make a move—take off on a strole for the dressinroom door. Almost there an I turn, shoot that messinger some eye talk.

Ain't hard t'get my story over. Watchin ever move I make. Picks up his drink an comes along, *eat*in me with his eyes.

Wanna have a little talk, find out jes what he got on his mind—this party in a motel an all. That's what I got on *my* mind.

But *him*, what he got on *his* mind—Ooh-wee! I look for *steam* any minit. Gee-zuz, he's feelin so feisty it's about t'come squirtin right out! Yeah!

Cause I go through that door an wait right inside there, in the dark, an direckly here goes him—in that door, sets his drink down on a shelf, an then he's all over me like outa some French movie I seen.

Don't know why he thinks he gotta pull this bit, *here!* Gee-zuz, baby, I can pick up the radiashun on my meddle telepathy—can *feel* what he got for me, he don't gotta make no demonstrashun. Yeah, cause I can feel if he's only puttin on, too. An he ain't puttin on. No! But all this maulin jes a waste a time. Can't go through with nothin here, in this Fish Pond.

So I cool it, jes stand there a-gin the wall real stone.

Don't let that feisty move me one bit. No, not even when he gets me in this bearhug an he's huffin away in my ear, Oh Kitten where you been so long—ooh Kitten what a fool I was that last time. You don't hold that against me, *do* you? *Please* don't hold that against me. An like that.

Pretty soon he sees he ain't movin me, an that slows him down.

Then I say, You, eh, finish?

Real nasty, way I say that. An him, he goes from red hot t'ice cold, that quick. Moves offa me an leans up a-gin the other wall, picks up his drink.

Well baby, I really didn't mean t'turn him off *that* much. All I was tryin t'do was keep from catchin his heat an losin my dum burrhead back here.

Anyhow, I move right on past that scene like it never happen, an I ast him what he got set up for this party. I say, Hey you tole me everthin's set. Now let's have some details, messinger.

Stands there real cold, don't say nothin for a time, jes sucks that drink. Then he say—jes's nasty's he can say it—say, You admires await the pleasure of you company, soon's you done here, I'll drive you out t'the motel, an—

An I cut him off. *What* motel?

Goes t'open his mouth on that, but me—like I'm haff mad at myseff, alla way mad at him, I say, Hey baby, *you* ain't drivin *me* out t *no* motel! That's the first thing I wanna get straight, you hear?

Like he gone stone deaf on me, never heard a word, goes on talk about how he gonna take me out t'this motel an gonna make it worth my while, an like that.

Got a boyfriend meetin me when the club close, an *he* gonna drive me out t'this motel. What I say.

Get a rise outa him with that. Yeah, I say boyfriend, an this messinger straightens his back. Oh no, he say, oh no you can't do *that.* Some other night it wouldn't make no diffrence, but t'night, he say, gotta perteck this other party's idenidy.

I tell him, Shove this other party's idenidy, I gotta perteck my ass. Gonna take along my boyfriend for insurance.

An him, here's him, comes on like a Jay Pee puttin down the law, say, *I'll* drive you out, an *I'll* take you home. You go with *me*, an that's *final*!

I say, Oh no, Hap goes along, waits outside in the car!

*No!* An *that's* the final *word!*

Up his final ass. Kee-ryess!

I say, You dum mothah, you wanna drive me out—yeah out, outa my mind! Won't even say *what* motel, won't let me bring along a bizness manager. I say, Forget it, baby, here. An I'm reachin in my pocketbook, gonna fish out that fifty an pertend I wanna give it back.

An right here—dingaling, round two. Here comes the man. Like outa nowhere. Open my mouth t'say somethin, an here he is. Say, What have we here?

I can't think of a word! Jes stand there with my mouth hangin open.

Man say, A little party?

I say, Oh yeah, little party. Only this . . . this . . . this john—

Man say, *Geegee!*

Never spose t'call 'em a john to they face. So I say,

This gentlemin wanna take me out t'some party in some motel, won't tell me *what* motel.

Man turn on that messinger an them two start yip-yappin. Tells the man all this crap about this very importint distingwish friend a his, an he say, *That's* why he can't say *what* motel.

Acts like he buyin all this, the man, an then he pull a switcheroo. Say, Okay let's go on in an give this other party a call, let Geegee talk t'*him*.

Messinger goes for this, so we go in dressinroom an he gets on the phone, pulls out this little a-dress book an dials. Meantime, the man pulls me over an he say, Don't worry. Go on out t'this party if you wanna. Later on I'll call, make sure you's okay.

I say, But how you gonna know where I'm *at?*

Don't worry, don't worry—what he say. We's tecknickly set up!

What he's tryin t'tell me is, in this club, even the bugs got bugs.

Anyhow, this other party's on the line now, an the messinger callin me over. I get on an I say, Hello?

Voice sound like a bullfrog at the bottom of a well say, *Looo?*

Humph! That's nowhere. So I say, You this very distingwish gentlemin friend a Jimmy?

Don't say nothin back for a long time, an then he say, Put Jay See back on, please.

An that, baby, is the sum cottinpickin total a that hello-hello. Jay See, Jimmy, that mothahfuggin messinger gets back on an they talk awhile, an I don't hang around t'lissen.

Due on stage, so me an the man go out an he give this speel on the new talent an all, an then I go on out an sing. What's new, an Teach me t'night.

Hey! That's a laugh.

Time I get back, Jimmy's gone an the man's waitin on me. He say, Geegee ole girl, you's marvellus! Now don't you worry about a *thing!* You jes go on with this john an leave it all up t'me.

Leave it up t'*him!* She-it!

But I tell him yeah sure okay, an I go on back out t'the bar, take up my same place tween these two johns I was with all along.

One of 'em takes one look at me an pulls out his hanky. I'm in a big sweat. Wipes my face with his hanky, an I thank him kindly, an we settle back down t'the innerestin conversashun an spit-back.

Settin there goin through this bit an the man comes up again, an he say, Geegee you ain't got a thing to worry about. I talk t'Sharmain an Wanda, an they boff been out with this john, an they say he's aye-okay. He say, An the name a this motel you goin is the Valley Vue, room two oh four. An I got the phone number, too, so don't worry. Say, You jes go on an make youseff a little side money.

Well baby, all this don't worry don't worry sure gives me the worries, but how m'I spose t'tell the man about the last time I had with this . . . this . . . Jay See. Keeryess! I ain't even gonna *try*.

So! Put in the time.

Can tell the way that bartender's lookin he's fixin t'ask me what happen, so I take off, circilate.

Feel easier about talkin t'that messinger now, so I'm on my way over t'see him, an guess what. Sharmain's gassin him. Yeah!

She's on him the rest a the night, too.

An then, closin time, Jimmy comes around an takes me by the arm an we sayin good-bye t'everbody an all—here goes that fuggin Sharmain, a-waddle-ass swishin over t'us with this big tommin black nanny grin all over her face, an she say, Good Luck, *Gaegae!*—that the silly-ass way she say it. An then she give that messinger a little squeeze an takes off wigglin her way along.

Liked t'break her back wigglin. An he's standin there takin it all in, this wigglin. So I say, Hey baby, you wanna swap girls?

Oh no, no no, he don't wanna do that.

Okay, come on.

She-it! He oughta take her. Jes his type. Phoney's a three dollah bill. Ain't got a real hair on her head, died 'em all orange. Hiyella, orange hair, phony aksent. Kee-ryess!

Anyhow, we's outside, I tell him t'hold it right here, gotta wait on my boyfriend, tell him.

He say no no, come on, the hell with him, but I lean him up a-gin the wall an we don't budge. Wants t'hold this buildin up like not a-tall, but we goddam well do wait. Oh yeah!

An pretty soon, here goes that Voltswagon down the other end a the block. Busy street. Hookers everwhere, workin boff sides. Cars all jammed up, lot a horn-blowin, big scene. Takes Hap a good while t'make it through this jam, but I don't move a stitch till he makes it.

Then I leave on the run, out in the street wavin an Hap pulls up. Stick my head down by the winda, an I say, Hello you confederit cunsugger, how's the white man's burden?

Jes a little inside joke, baby, don't pay it no mind.

Then I say, Lissen Couzin, gotta put off that celebrashun a little while, cause I got a couple live ones. Goin out t'some motel call the Valley Vue, room two oh four. You got that? Two oh four. So follow me out an wait right near by.

An Hap, that sumbitch, guess what he say. Say, *How much?*

She-it. Knowed that'd be the first thing he'd say. But I act real surprise. Say, Couzin! Don't you *love* me? You gonna worry about *money* more'n you worry about *me?*

*How much!*

Well I got fifty so far, gonna make another fifty when I get there. At least!

That lights Hap up, but that's all the time we got, cause Jimmy bearin down on us now, an this car behind the Voltswagon honkin away like he's flippin his lid.

So I wave good-bye an take off down the street with that messinger.

Puts me in a Thunderbird. Red an white, leather seats, the whole bit.

Take off, cruise up t'the stoplight, it's on red an that gives Hap a chance t'swing around an get behind.

Then I try t'make a little conversashun. Hey baby, this a nice car, you must be doin all right. What's you hussle?

Say, *What?*

I mean, where you work at now, huh?

Gee-zuz, it could be somebody else's car, I'm jes givin the mothah a chance t'sound off big deal.

But he don't. Tells me he works for the coundy now, an he say this like he's shamed or mad, or somethin.

Me, I stick in there tryin, I say, Wow, must pay real good, huh?

But that jes shuts him up tight. Don't say another motherin word the whole trip.

Feelin awful strong about somethin. You can see that by his face.

She-it! What the hell's *he* got t'be mad about?

Queers the whole ride.

Dam near, but I don't let it bug me, jes set back an go with it—ground sailin by, an that big full moon standin still up there. Cuttin right inta the night with them headlights—I go all this.

An my heart even goes out t'*him*, too.

Trouble is, no matter how much *I'm* for goin out, he ain't gonna pick it up inside *him*. Too fulla mad, I spose. Ain't got no room left on his meddle telepathy.

But he's drivin okay—that's one good thing—an Hap's comin along good, too, so I don't worry.

Not a peep outa him till we pull up t'this motel, an he say, Here we are!

All lit up out front like a crissmiss tree. Drive on back where it's dark an he wheels that Bird to a swingin stop, bumps the curb an makes it take a little bow, right in front a room two oh four.

An then he comes on like a radio commershul, he

say, Now don't be afraid a racial discriminashun here, Kitten, cause I know the managemin!

Yeah, that's what he say—*I* don't gotta be afraid cause *he* know the managemin!

She-it, baby. I take a breath an I'm all set t'put this ofay straight on a whole lotta things—an then I jes let that breath go—*Pheeew!*

Kee-ryess, I could gas off all night on race, let him know jes *who's* afraid a *what*, gas off all night an never muss his hair.

So all I say is, Managemin ain't gonna discriminate on *my* skin, cause you *know* 'em, eh.

An he say, Yeah. Then he say, An we got the best room in the place, too—a whole family sweet!

Well, la-dee-dah! How bout that!

Hey, what a sweet family *we* make, huh!

In case there are those of you who fail to comprehend the board head's infatuation with Kitten—especially don't comprehend it carrying him to the point where money became no object—let me say this:

Frankly, neither do I. I didn't comprehend it at the time, and now, looking back on it, I remain at a loss to explain it. To justify his motivations. For Mr. Pennypacker was a man deeply involved in the affairs of his time. He was, in fact, at the center of the Hook County political hurricane. And being so deeply involved in politics is not conducive to making one vulnerable to sexual excesses, nor wanderings from the path of faithful matrimony. Plus the fact that in politics there are these relations with other politicians, which keep one quite busy.

Therefore, I am really at a loss to explain Mr. Chairman's raging motivations. On top of this, by the time I got Kitten to the motel, he had fallen asleep!

Well, he had said he planned to take a little catnap, yes. But the depth of his slumber, when we arrived, was such that I am tempted to the suspicion that he may have taken a sleeping pill.

Which, come to think of it, may have had a definite influence on what happened to him later.

However, I don't wish to leap ahead of myself. First things first.

And, what I did first was try to get Kitten to go immediately into the bedroom with him. Which she flatly refused to do!

Because of what she did do, I feel strongly compelled to tell you that even though I've put off my marriage, I am not a case of a strangulated libido, nor do I eschew the simple natural sexual function. In fact, my fiancée and I have had pre-marital intercourse—being modern enough to have chosen a doctor to supervise us in this, to instruct, advise, and guide us. He outfitted Barbara with a diaphragm and discussed with me the sensitive parts of a woman's anatomy and how the woman plays the passive role in sex and so has to be aroused by foreplay, and the man must know all the techniques, etc., and above all be extremely patient and not let himself get carried away. And we are, as our doctor put it, healthy, intelligent young adults, and therefore capable of achieving a normal sex life, despite having to put off marriage a year or so for financial reasons.

Not that our relationship is mercenary. Because both our families agree that, right now while I'm establishing my career and working to achieve an annual take-home of $15,000, because, after all, we both come from home environments where we're used to things—things which can't even be contemplated on less than $15,000.

But don't get the idea from this that we're materialistic. It's just that we're sensible and practical. You see so many tragic mistakes these days—young couples marrying right out of high school or college, before they have an adequate income. It only stands to reason that such marriages are doomed to failure.

I *know* . . . I'm perfectly aware of the fact that most marriages fail due to sexual incompatibility. But how can you gain sexual compatibility and achieve satisfying coitus on an inadequate income?

Besides which, Barbara's father is firmly convinced that a tour of Europe will round out her education. She had an unfortunate period during her college days when she seemed tempted by certain communist-tinged criticisms of America, so her father quite wisely knows that when she sees how backward Europe is, she'll come home with a deeper appreciation of America—our roads, modern schools, the success of our corporations, the efficiency of our police, etc.

However, what I'm driving at is this: that while she is in Europe . . .

But let me render this a different way. I'll do it by

telling you exactly what she said to me at the airport the day she flew to Paris. "Jim," she said, "if you need sex while I'm in Europe, buy it! Please buy it," she said, "so you won't get into any troublesome involvements."

So, you see, we're a very modern couple with a very avant-garde view toward sex. Ergo, a woman *can't* have extra-marital affairs because she's the bearer of children, but that's no reason for the man to do without while she's away. Because, as our doctor pointed out, a woman's sexual urge is not as urgent as a man's, and there are times when a man *needs* it.

But wait a minute! Don't jump to the conclusion that *I* contemplated buying sex from Kitten! Let me put you straight on that extremely important point right now!

Even though I've already mentioned that I did not—repeat did not—induce her to have relations, it's important that I make this matter crystal clear. And clarity, as our advertising industry has proven, is the result of repetition. So bear with me, Dear Reader, while I reiterate on this matter of Mr. Pennypacker's buying sex from Kitten while I stood by and never so much as took off my suitjacket. For it becomes very important, finally. Ergo, there occurs a happening which might indicate that I, had I lust for Kitten, might have implicated myself. Albeit, if it had been my idea to bring her to that motel, you might gather that what happened was, in some roundabout way, perhaps, *my* fault. Which it wasn't.

Oh, I'll admit that there might have been a time. . . . Three years ago I might have found her attractive. In a purely animalistic way, purely physical. But since then I've matured and developed and vastly improved my taste in women. No longer am I satisfied with simple bestiality. Sure, it's necessary once in awhile to hire a girl to satisfy one's baser instincts, but it's stupid to lose sight of the higher rewards to be gained from *social* intercourse—i.e., with young women of family standing.

And I have an apartment near the Courthouse which is simply ideal for entertaining women of taste and cultivation, and will not shirk from disclosing to you that I attract virtual bevies of young ladies. Why, just the other night, five of them paid me a surprise visit—among them being a very brilliant Vassar grad from one of this area's foremost industrial families, plus a local celebrity, a girl who was a Miss America contestant, not so many years ago.

Well, we had a most stimulating discourse (albeit accompanied by two pitchers of martinis and, of course, some twisting) and two of them even did some shopping for me: I dispatched them to a local butcher shop and they came back with thick, juicy sirloins for all, which another pair of them charcoaled on my roof-terrace grill. And that evening, which lasted well into the wee hours, did *not*, as some might think, turn into drunken debauchery. Our intercourse was lively, but it was strictly on the *social* level—e.g., our exchanges were of an oral nature. That is to say, *verbal*. On a verbal plane.

There was only one drawback: some practical joker in the crowd who stole a case of scotch. It must have been June, the Vassar girl, come to think of it. As a joke, of course, for surely all her wants are well taken care of, being from the family she's from.

However, lest I stray from the true course of this narrative, what I'm driving at is the fact that, with the phone numbers of a couple of really high-class party girls (both of them entertainers at the Fish Pond, incidentally), and with the permission of my beloved, and on top of this, with the company of such stimulating young women of family background and education, I am not, in the least, tempted by the likes of Kitten. Which has nothing whatsoever to do with her race or color. Nor with any signs of impotence or latent homosexuality in me. It's simply that I do not, any longer, wish to avail myself of some girl from a Negro bordello, mainly because of the danger of venereal disease.

So I did not make advances. And rumors to the contrary from any source whatsoever are pure fantasy of the worst and most malicious sort, and if you want to go to court about it I'll prove perjury. Because I was there in that motel for one reason, and one reason only: namely, to see to it that the Chairman received, for the ridiculously large sum he was paying, satisfaction for his money; ergo, I was there as a disinterested party, to make sure she didn't take advantage of his large generosity, the way she did once with me. And she was there to sell her sex—to the board head, not to me—and I never touched her!

Well, of course, you understand that when I say I didn't *touch* her, I am not being absolutely and completely literal. What I'm trying to convey is that I didn't get undressed and go to bed with her.

Naturally, the way she was behaving, I had to do something: i.e., I was forced, finally, to handle her, so to speak. Which is not to say that I stripped off my clothes and entered into any meaningful sexual congress with her, the sort she seemed adamant in trying to provoke. No such thing! I never so much as unbuttoned my suitjacket, as mentioned.

I did, in fact, go to some lengths to avoid her, even when she attempted some of the most mentally sick vamping tactics I've ever seen—e.g., by stripping stark naked right before my very eyes!

Oh yes, I know the nudity of the female has been sanctioned by the Supreme Court, in magazines, etc., but as we all know, the high court under Earl Warren has degenerated terribly. This matter being but one instance of that degeneration. Because, obviously, the nudity of such Negro prostitutes as Kitten, and done with an intent to excite to licentiousness, is perverse and even verges on the neurotic.

About which, more later.

He plops down at one end an I plop down at the other.

We's in the sittin room, an they got a bedroom too. The other one's in there sleepin. Can hear him snorin.

Don't say nothin, jes set there starin. I'm starin at him an he's starin at the floor.

Feel a little warm, so I stand up and take off my vynal jacket, lay it over the back a the chair.

Then he stands up an takes off his topcoat—real careful, like he's fraid he gonna tear it up, he ain't careful.

I say, Gee Sweetie, that's a nice coat.

Puttin on, tryin t'get a thing goin.

He smiles an holds it up, say, Made in Hongkong. Pats it an smooths it down—Kee-ryess, baby, he's like lovin it up! Carry it over t'the closit an pulls out a hanger, then he turn on me an say, They don't make coats like this *here!* Labor's price itseff outa the competishun!

I say, Yeah.

Don't know what the fug he's talkin bout, but I say yeah.

Workin it over the hanger, he say, Notice the seem. Turns it inside out and holds it up.

Ooh yeah, wow, gee, sure do got a seem. That's me.

He say, That's real workminship for you. Hand made!

An I mean, baby, he's high on what he's sayin. Eyes jes a-lightin up the whole room.

Gets it hung up, an I figure we's over that topcoat bit, so I say, How about you suitcoat, baby—made in Hongkong too?

Swings around on me an this time he's hot. No! Course not! It's Eyetalian!

Oh, oh yeah sure, Eyetalian. That's me. You gonna take it off an hang it up?

Gives me this real long hard look. Guess he jes woke up I'm puttin him on. Anyhow, he don't say a word, don't take it off. Goes back over an sets down at his end a the room an then he goes into this slow, hard starin at me.

She-it! I don't know whether to laugh or go blind! Really, baby, gettin unner his skin sorta tickles me. Lot better'n havin him come on with me like I ain't even people. Maybe he keeps on that hard lookin he gonna see *me.*

Ha! Hardly! Can tell by the way he lookin, all he

seein is my color an my sex. The up front, what he seein. Past that, this mothah's on guess work. An that wouldn't be so bad—if he'd quit believin his own guesses.

Anyhow, gives me a good long stare, an then he turns t'starin at the floor again, an we's back t'start.

This ain't the same trick I remember, comin on so big in that cathouse. He ain't movin on automatic no more. No soul.

I mean, baby, I don't go this lily white church bit, like god's a beard they paint on a winda an all that, but you don't gotta go through that routine t'know how t'feel soul, cause I can be at the other end of a room an do that.

Is what scares me with this mothah—hard's he starin at me, he ain't sendin *out* nothin with all that eye-work, an you wanna know why? Lost it. Yeah, lost it, chase it away, or somethin.

Well that ain't real hard t'do. Been feelin close t'losin my own seff lately. Cause sometimes havin it's a pain in the ass. Makes you tolerate people won't even *try* t'tolerate you.

Anyhow, what I'm sayin, back t'start.

I take about all this settin an starin I can, then I get up an walk over an hold out my hand. Looks up like he don't know what I'm after. He knows. I keep my hand out an pretty soon he stands up, goes fishin in his pocket an pulls out some bills—two twennies an a ten.

Okay, I'm back on the other side pertendin I'm shovin them bills in my purse. Really, baby, I got this little pocket in my bra, is where I jam them bambinos, but I make it look like I shove 'em down in my purse.

Then, like bein fifty dollahs lighter kinda loosen up his

face a minit, an he say, Well Kitten, I don't know *what* t'say—I didn't count on him fallin asleep!

The distingwish. Still snorin.

So I quick say, Oh don't worry bout that, baby, me an you can have us a good time an forget all about him.

Gives me this bad uppity look, so I switch around an say, An *then* I can take care a *him!* When he wakes up.

That's better.

Gee-zuz! What a drag! Way he was comin on in the club I was sure it'd be a movin scene in this motel. Now what the hell's the holdup?

Settin, starin, lissenin t'the snorin. Kee-ryess! Gives me the jitters. Why don't he take a notion, make a start?

Three year ago he had more fuggin notions'n he had sense. Sure was a-startin then. Oh yeah! Back then we had a start. For jes a little while.

Trouble was, we didn't get that start t'go nowhere. I mean about the time we got goin—the end! I didn't have enough sense t'get the price straight with him when I shoulda, an after he got his an wasn't gonna pay up.

Got my money, this time. Yeah. Right here keepin warm in my bra—jes a little slit on the inside, can slip five or six bills in there an you can't even see a rumple. Pretty neat, huh?

Anyhow, what I'm sayin, we set there so long, I kinda slip off daydreamin. Was goin over the time I made it with him, back in my partmin.

But I don't no more'n dream off number one, he pipes up, say, Only one thing t'do, Kitten—go on in there an wake him up!

Huh?

Say, Go on, wake him up an do you stuff. An make it good too, cause I gave you top billin. An he goes on talkin how *later*, after his friend *leaves*, me an him'll be a*lone!*

An that's when I see what's goin on with *him*. Stretchin his pants so hard it liked t'poke a hole an come poppin out.

That's one thing, that hardon. Nother thing, that look he's givin me. Teeth tight t'gether, even when he's talkin. Comin on me with this wild-ass hot look now, on top a his mad look.

I say t'myseff, Girl you wanna end up alone in this goddam motel with *that?*

Kee-ryess! I ain't goin in that bedroom first—end up stuck here with this messinger. Gee-zuz! I been *there* be*fore!* Gonna take care a *him* first, *then* go in the bedroom.

Take the feisty outa him, leave the other one in there sleepin, an then after I take care a the sleeper, I can split an keep away from whatever fancy ideas that mothah got bouncin around in his ofay mind.

Cause really baby, it don't take much meddle telepathy t'see this daddy got *some*thin crankin away inside his head. I can jes feel the air goin thicker by the minit, an there for jes a second—him settin at one end an me at the other—we's puttin eyes on each other so hard it's like we's wired up t'gether. Gives me a spooky feelin, like the walls fallin away an I'm out way off in some lonely nowhere place with this mothahfuggah bearin down on me, nowhere t'run.

So I cut that wire, stand up an do a couple mashpotata

steps. Then I say, Hey baby, turn down them lamps an stop lookin at me that way, huh?

Jes keeps a-lookin, tells me t'go on in the bedroom an take care a the bored head.

Me, I say, First Lover, I'm gonna take care a *you*. You the one *needs* it. Bored head's *sleep*in!

Stands up an puts his arm around my shoulder an he say, Do like I tole you, come on. Pushin me at the bedroom, but I kinda lean back on him an coax a little.

He's pushin an I'm leanin, an then his hands start slidin. Slide down my front, busy all the way, takes ahold a my dress an liffs it up over my head. Alla time tellin me t'go—go on in the bedroom.

I give him some help pullin my dress off. Can feel his breath ticklin my hair. Still talkin me inta the bedroom an pushin, but he ain't movin me no place cause I'm still jes a-leanin back on him. Yeah, he's pushin east an I'm leanin west, an we ain't goin nowhere. Only thing goin is his hands, an they's all over.

Then he say, Don't *temp* me, Kitten!

She-it! *Me* temp *him!* Ha! This daddy's hands what tempin *him*. Yeah! Them hands so busy now I'm scared he's gonna squeeze the money, pop right outa my bra.

So I move away on him, an I say, Hey baby, set down a minit an let me show ya somethin.

He don't like me movin away like that, sets there givin me that bad eye again, real stone. I mean, that's what he's puttin on up front.

I'm puttin on I'm a stripteazer carryin my dress, an I jes step over at him, hummin an beeboppin my own tune, an drop that dress on top a his head.

He grabs it, balls it up an throws it—sails right over me an lands in some corner back in the dark.

Didn't go much for the way he done that, but I keep on this kick, puttin on I'm a stripteazer. Gets to him pretty quick too, cause nex thing I know he's got his dingus out. I say, Yeah baby, give that thing a little air an maybe he'll come around an see things *my* way.

Anyhow, I got three eyes on me now. Playin t'the third one, still on this stripper routine an tossin in a little belly dance in memry of Sharmain. Take off my bra an toss it in his face—how bout that for livin fearless! An he balls that bra up an throws it t'hell an gone back behind the sofa.

Time out. I go over an make sure my money's okay after that throw, an I say—like I'm hurt—say, Gee Honey, *why* you throwin my *stuff* around like that, *huh?*

Aw Kitten, *please!* Go inta the bedroom, *please!*

Say that like he's got a pain.

She-it. Like I can't unnerstand a word he sayin. Come out from behind that sofa with a continental, an then I crack inta some twistin, go over and shake it down on him, see what that'll fetch.

Not much. Makes me out pretty nutty, is all, dancin around with no music. So I quit that dancin.

Take off a stockin, walk over an drop it down on him, an we's back t'playin our game—balls that stockin up an sails it off some place.

Same with the other stockin an my pants, balls 'em up an throws 'em away.

I say, Okay Lover, your turn, you do me a little strip-teaze now, come on. An I take ahold a his hand—real easy, like I'm only gonna pull him up offa the chair.

Well baby, that did it! Yeah. That action's what made the party.

Stripteaze? Oh no, uh uh. Surprise surprise. Me with my clothes off, an him with his clothes on! I mean—dig what happen—I give a little pull—not hard, jes a small one—an he come risin up like sap in the springtime, outa that chair an all over me. Got one hand wrapped around my back an the other one helpin his lips find where t'kiss. Nex thing I know, he's layin me down in a pile-up on the floor. Yeah, he leans on me an I land smack plop on my bare blackass an he's right there on top, an before I know which end is up, we's all carried away, ridin off at a huff-edy-puff. Cause he's up my lazy river makin great big waves! Didn't give me a chance, was in me that quick. In me an goin t'town about the time my butt touch the floor, and aye-way we goddam well do go. Kee-ryess!

I knowed this daddy warm for my form, but—like, *too much*. Didn't know he's runnin no high feever. Gee-zuz! He so hot he jes goes all up through me like radiashun. No stoppin it, jes up and up an inta my blood, an straight t'my head, an by that time I'm outa my motherin mind! Yeah! Me, like a dum cottin patch conkubine, I forget everthin—lose my head from all that radiashun an jes turn loose an ride that rod the whole way home.

An you wanna know somethin? I never made it home no sooner. Cross my heart I didn't. No sir. I mean we sure did find us a shortcut, cause jes about the time I catch the heat his cock sendin out, he's windin up big and strokin, an then that strokin took me over an I was *gone!* Ooh-wee! I mean that hotrod jes pick me up an put me right on that everlovin rockabye ride, an the nex thing I know, I'm cruisin in on automatic, bringin this mothahfuggin messin-ger more'n he could ever *hope* t'buy.

Yeah! He ain't *never* gonna have *that* much money!

An I can't for the life a me figure out how that sumbitch wound me up an got my goodies like that. Hotrod or no hotrod. Gee-zuz! Baby, I had hot ones bef*ore!* Been in this rackit over three year now, so you know dam right well hot tricks ain't no new thing with *this* girl—right?

Yeah, an on top a that, Hap's right outside waitin—he *better* be—an me an him got big plans—celebrashun. That's the worst part, this mothahfuggin messinger cut right inta what I was savin up for Hap. Took the fine edge off, an maybe he even queered the whole scene. Kee-ryess! I wasn't plannin on makin it with no *trick!*

That goddam twoit a mine's the big fugup—had a need for Hap an let it go on this bastid, jes took over an stole the show. Throbbin away there for a time like she was tryin t'go an get me pregnent.

Anyhow, layin there, gettin back my sense, tryin t'find out what's goin on here.

And that ain't no easy thing, baby, cause here's me down on the bottom naked's a jaybird, an here's him up on top, clothes on—them goddam buttons diggin inta me, an that suit liked t'rub my skin raw. An sides that, this mothah got my ear in his mouth.

Better make a change here. Life's too short t'lay like this —right? Unner some ofay sumbitch with his clothes rub-bin you skin an his mouth blowin all over you ear. I mean I had enough a this shiddy bit right now, soon's I come t'my senses.

So I give a roll and a belly hump, get him offa me an we's layin side by side.

Look over, an here's him, layin there with his mouth wide open, pantin away an starin at the ceilin. Like maybe he's havin hiseff a revelashun or somethin, so I don't do nothin for a minit, jes lay there lookin at him.

Then he say, Ah'*hem!* An he sorta come out of it, close his mouth an looks at me.

An me—like how could I mess up so *bad?*—an in such a short time? Baby, that's somethin I don't *know*, but I did. Oh yeah! Cause what I done, I try t'come on human with this bastid. I say, *Wow*, did I ever *come!*

An you know what he does? Gives me this real mean look, kinda chews his teeth like, an he jes lay there givin me this hateful goddam eye-work.

Well baby, I'm so surprise I don't know what t'*do*. Don't know how t'come back on that *look!*

All I can do for a long time is jes lay there lookin deep inta them blue eyes wonderin how in the mad-ass mothah-fuggin world can this sumbitch be so *cun*-temtible! So *cold!* So sad-ass sadistick! I mean, he was cuntemtible bef*ore*, but *now!* What's his trouble *now?*

Sits up an puts his back on me, an then he gets on his feet, slow, like he can hardly make it up. Walks over back t'his chair an parks his ass again. Then he looks down on me, an this time he's kinda smilin.

Well how bout that! I say t'myseff, Baby maybe this daddy did find hiseff some heart after all. Maybe he like got back a little *soul* from that piece.

Oh no. Uh-uh. That ain't it a-tall! No, cause nex peep outa him, he say, You came, eh?

He still kinda smilin—shiddy, like, but smilin. So I say, Yeah baby, real big!

Then he laughs, like small an mean, *Heay heay heay*.

An I'm hip. Thinks he's a big deal stud or somethin. Stands there puttin on this big stud bit, sticks his wornout bird back in his pants, zips up, sits down.

Gee-zuz! I shoulda hit him with a long, loud piece a my mind, but I was jes too jumped out. Bout all I could do, once I got hip t'this *heay heay heay*, is pick myseff off that floor an make it t'the baffroom, take a towel an wipe my bottom.

Then—like I didn't even plan it—I carry that towel back out an throw it in his face. Hard!

*Heay heay heay*. That's all I get back for that towel.

Walk over an set myseff down on my side, an we's back t'start. Again.

Stares at me for a time, an then he say, Okay Kitten, now go on in the bedroom an make it good. I want you at you *best* in there, unnerstand?

Gee-fuggin-kee-ryess-all-mighty! He *must* be outa his skull! I don't know what t'say. Set there with my jaw hangin, wonderin how he got t'be so mothahfuggin far gone deep lost.

Don't jes *sit* there, *move!* That's him.

Me, I keep it right where it is, don't move an inch.

Then, hard's I try not to, had a tear come t'my eye, had t'get up an fetch that towel an wipe 'em away. Grab that towel off the floor, went carryin it inta the bedroom wipin my eye.

Don't get me wrong, baby, I didn't take no cryin jag. Wasn't feelin sorry for myseff, neither. Was jes a couple small tears an I don't know *why*. I was so mad at that cuntemtible bastid, an *still*—I mean, how he can love up that topcoat like he done—how he can do *that!*

Well I know where he lost hiseff at—I mean, I know where his soul's at. Put it in the closit with his topcoat. Yeah!

But why should *I* drop a tear over *that?*

There are certain times when certain ancient and enduring truths are . . . well, you might say, acted out symbolically. Have you ever noticed—in your *own* life?

For instance, one day I was standing on a corner downtown waiting to cross the street and some old lady, a pedestrian, who was also waiting to cross, just stepped off the curb and began toddling across—with the Do Not Walk light glaring right down in her face. And then some university student came whipping around the corner in a low-slung foreign job, trying to make the corner before the amber changed to a redlight. Which—his haste—is why he didn't notice the old lady, who was disobeying the pedestrian light in an attempt to beat the same amber traffic light.

Well, the sportscar's bumper—I saw this all very clearly and coolly and therefore have a surprising degree of total recall, can see it all once again in my mind right now—the bumper caught the old lady in the shins and toppled her like a tenpin in a bowling alley. There was even a moment when she was literally suspended in midair and the sportscar was roaring on under her. It was halfway to the end of the block when she came down—*splat!*—and landed, precisely on the spot in the street where her shin had made initial contact with that bumper.

Of course the student got his car stopped and came back and there was a great to-do about it all, with some people trying to tell the traffic officer exactly what happened, and some others, me among them, trying to move on and get away from there so we wouldn't end up losing valuable time in traffic court as witnesses.

Anyway, what I'm pointing out here is that very ancient and enduring Truth about the irresistible force and the immovable object. Because that sportscar was going hellbent for election and that little old lady, poor soul, could hardly get around, let alone be nimble enough to jump back in time to let that sportscar miss her.

All of which is by way of introducing what happened between Kitten and myself. You see, she just couldn't accept the idea that I did not intend to buy sex from her and that my sole purpose was to negotiate the transaction between she and the board head. Like that little old lady, she just couldn't wait for the light to change, so to speak, couldn't accept my signal, and took off illegally jay-walking.

Not that I'm trying to put *all* the blame on her for what *did* happen! Because, like that sportscar trying to make it around the corner before the light changed, I played my part in the accident, too.

Now, when I told you, Dear Reader, as I believe you may recall my having done, that I had not, at that time, so much as touched her, I wasn't storying to you. Because like that little sportscar, I was halfway down the block, figuratively speaking, before I realized. And by that time, of course, it was too late!

But you're probably wondering what did happen. Well, frankly, I'm not altogether certain. The driver of that sportscar had to rely on spectators to tell *him*, but in *my* case, there weren't any spectators. The Chairman, you see, was asleep.

As nearly as I can piece it together, what happened was this: Kitten, like that little old lady trying to jaywalk, tempted fate too far. By her stripping and provoking and prancing around, etc. And, like that little sportscar whipping around the corner, the accident was over before I knew it. I never so much as even loosened my necktie, it happened so quickly.

Which is not to say that I didn't try to prevent it. For I did try, and desperately. I kept pushing her—gently, at first, then harder and harder, until, at one point, she actually fell to the floor. I really didn't mean to get so rough with her but why in the world wouldn't she take *no* for an answer? If she'd only done as I told her and gone straight into the bedroom and awakened Mr. Pennypacker and plied her foul trade, our accident would never have occurred.

But it did occur. Oh yes, it really did. And I'm afraid it stunned her almost as much as it stunned me. After it was all over—at which juncture I found myself lying on the floor beside her . . . you see, after I pushed her and she fell, I attempted to bring her to her feet—a mistake, because to tell the honest truth, when I reached down to assist her, she pulled and I came down right on top of her.

*Sic*, after it was all over, I found myself lying on the floor beside her and the expression on her face was . . . well, it was disturbed, if you know what I mean—sort of pained, you might say. But, as any right-thinking individual knows, she brought it all on herself, that accident—she'd been jaywalking just as surely as that old lady—and I was totally involved, when the accident occurred, in attempting to convince her that such brazen tactics as stripping were not only uncalled for, but entirely unappreciated, and had it not been for a weird coincidence of time and circumstances, I really feel I would have gotten through to her and meaningfully communicated, and that our accident would have been prevented. Therefore, for me to say that I absolutely did not touch her—i.e., that I had no relations with her at all—is not the God's honest and entire truth. But it is, really, the truth of my honest intentions. Albeit, our contact was but a momentary mistake, the culmination of several smaller mistakes made previously, and over and above this mistake, standing as a testimony to my honest intentions, is the hard fact that I never took off even one stitch of clothing.

But enough of that. I don't want this account to sound

as if I'm trying to justify myself. I don't *have* to justify myself.

More pertinent here would be my mystification—a point I believe it might prove enlightening to explain. You see, Kitten—during the aforementioned accident—had . . . well, to put it bluntly, an orgasm. Though I certainly won't stoop to a blow by blow rendering of how this much of the mystery occurred, naturally.

But there's a greater mystery. Where *it* came in was afterwards: ergo, she tended, at first, to be elated—but to such a degree that I became, quite frankly, a bit worried. She had, after all, achieved orgasm with insufficient fore-play—strange enough in itself. Following which, she distinctly revealed herself to be a neurotic manic-depressive by reverting to an abject dejection. Even a scarcely concealed hostility.

Which, of course, is very mysterious, because in all one's experience with women, has one ever found one who reacted to the supreme sexual acme *that* way? By first turning herself into a virtual vibrating machine and then, finally, by just lying there, sad? In a state of depression and, yes, even repressed hostility?

But perhaps I have failed to fully consider our racial differences. Maybe therein lies the answer to the riddle of her mysterious behavior.

At any rate, I did, finally, manage to get her into the bedroom with the soundly sleeping Mr. Chairman, at which point I was free to settle back in an easy chair and listen to some piped-in music. Folk songs symphonically rendered.

And to take my mind off the rather sordid scene this

evening of coincidence and accident had become, I focused my attention on the real involvement of my life—a matter far, far from what, I assumed, had temporarily captured the board head's attention. Namely, I was thinking of a little happenstance I may have neglected to mention . . . specifically, although I did refer to it indirectly when I cited that piece of Leftist legislation proposed by our Welfare Department—ergo, the $3,000 giveaway for those so-called unemployables, allegedly, but in reality, lazy dolts who lack the initiative to go out in the world and find themselves an employer to serve. What I didn't mention was that Herman—besides leading the fight to defeat this proposal—was also leading a movement to do away with the Public Relations Department.

*Sic*, to do away with *me!*

Yes, the esteemed Chairman had, of late, been talking up the abolition of PR. In this connection, it was stoutly rumored that the five-man majority faction, *led* by Mr. Pennypacker, was actually in *favor* of said abolition.

Let me spell it out for you. The board head, since he was unable to get his District Chairman's son into my job, had decided to do away with the *job*. With the entire County Public Relations function!

Well, as you can well imagine, this was a most unsavory thought. But wily old J.C., never one to say die, had, as of this late hour, created a way to nip said abolition movement in the bud. Because, you see, Mr. Pennypacker's awareness had, by now, shifted with dead certainty to the realization that the entire majority faction's very welfare was dependent on PR.

This point had been driven home to him, you see, beginning with my having taken it upon my own creative initiative to investigate and report upon a matter much more urgent than the abolition of PR, and one which is infinitely closer to the eminent board head's heart—e.g., the cancerous growth of welfarism. That is to say, if I could demonstrate for Herman, as I'm sure my report did demonstrate, that Public Relations is, in actual and indisputable fact, an indispensable function, a long strong arm of government which he and the other members of the majority faction could—granted—do without . . . just like they could do without insurance on their wives, homes, and cars. Ergo, at their own peril! If I could get this across to him on terms he could accept—as my report most certainly did do—I would enjoy the support of the entire majority faction and, when my trial period in this position ends in January, I would get my contract, assuring my continuance for two full years.

Therefore, the defeat of that proposal put forward by those wild-eyed comsymps in Welfare, due to come before the board at Monday's meeting, was the big skyhook from which hung the career of one James Cartwright Holland, especially if you realize how difficult it becomes to counter such newspaper sensationalism as Welfare's sobbing tactics stirred up. Because, you see, recent yellow journalism had cast the majority faction in a bad light, and they were left with no response other than the obvious one—that such legislation carries welfarism much too far, and is simply more evidence of our internal menace: creeping socialism.

Which obvious fact seems difficult for some Americans to grasp. Sadly but truly we are, I fear, some of us, politically naïve, and therefore vulnerable, at times, to the clever devices employed by those who have been duped by the hate-mongering Left and its insidious liberal propaganda.

But my report, crammed full of real factual data as it was, would counteract all that, including those twisted accounts given by our pliable press corps as it swayed before Welfare's methods like so many twigs in a hurricane. The gist of it being that, even though it's generally good business to rehabilitate the poor, make them into cash customers, etc., there are *some* people in this County who are simply beyond reclamation. Because my investigation showed conclusively that the alleged unemployables in question were, in fact:

A) Employable

B) Unemployed because they couldn't hold down decent jobs, and this sad fact for such ridiculous reasons as:

1. Unpunctuality
2. Resentment of supervision
3. Failure to work well with others

And their color has nothing to do with it; they're just a lot of drunken riff-raff, not at all incapacitated, but just too stubborn to adjust to modern urban or suburban living. To substantiate this, I had shown how some of them were fresh off small farms they had failed to even soil-bank at a profit. Thus, they were, my report concluded:

A) Not Hook County's responsibility in the first place

B) Especially not our Welfare Department's concern, since not covered by existing local ordinances

C) Simply too lazy to pick up and move on and find suitable jobs, and therefore a psychiatric problem, which takes them out of our jurisdiction entirely and puts them smack into the hands, and at the mercy of, whatever federal bureaucrats make their parasitic living catering to such maladjustments.

Another important point I must reiterate, repeat, and stress is this: that the board head had expressed great enthusiasm for my report. At dinner, and later at the Fish Pond. He had thanked me profusely and had said in no uncertain terms that my report virtually doomed Welfare's proposal, and he had gone to some lengths to tell me that I should make a major effort to inform the press of the facts my report presented—gleaned, as they were, from the files of prominent businessmen and industrialists.

Thus, victory was in the bag, practically—both for the Chairman at Monday's board meeting, and for yours truly in January.

And I've endeavored to bring all this to your attention—that mishap with Kitten and the matter of my report—not to boast of my effectiveness in either public relations or sex relations, but so that you will comprehend, clearly, the profound shock I felt, the deeply penetrating disturbance caused in me when I discovered moments later that the Chairman . . .

But wait. I leap ahead of myself. Let me put all this in the proper sequence for you.

The first phase of which was that, just as I thought she might, Kitten tried to pull a fast one.

Set down on the edge a that bed, pull myseff t'gether.

Distingwish gentlemin layin on his side, snorin up a storm. Ain't missed a beat all night.

Gee-zuz! I knowed them Decent people sleep good, but *this*'s reediculous!

Don't know how I'm gonna take care a this one. Ain't for tryin t'figure it out. Too tired. Downright whupt.

Jes set there on the edge a the bed an lissen t'that rough tough lily-white mothah in the other room movin around.

He turns on some kinda dum nothin music, so I'm settin here lissenin t'that an the distingwish snorin.

Then I get up an sorta mope around this room. Got a long mirrer on the closit door in here an they's enough light comin in from the other room so's I can see myseff, an I'm jes standin there lookin myseff over.

Don't look nothin like how I feel. Feel whupt an tired an all jumped out inside, but it don't even show in that mirrer. Girl lookin back at me looks wide awake an a little frantic.

Stand there tryin t'make myseff look back like how I feel, but I ain't gettin nowhere. Never do. Funny thing, I never seem t'look in the mirrer like how I feel I oughta look. I mean, one time I come on some mirrer feelin strong's the worl's champiun, an sometimes like a pretty little round-face baby, but in that mirrer I'm the same ole girl starin back out, don't matter how I feel.

Maybe that means somethin. Yeah, maybe it means the same thing's them nightmares I been havin lately—other night I dream some big tall buildin was fallin down on me an I caught it an held it there, kep it from squashin me, but then I remember, in my dream, how I can't do that, hold up some big buildin. An soon's I remember that, buildin came down an I woke up.

But this ain't no time for figurin out dreams an stuff. Got this distingwish t'figure out. Still snorin away.

An if that messinger thinks *I'm* gonna spoil his good sleep, he's outa his mind! What I do is, I take a notion—little nap won't do *me* no harm neither—an I go round t'crawl in bed beside this big mothah an rest up. Yeah, an then I can hop out an get dress, tell that messinger bye-bye, be in that Voltswagon an on down that hiway fore he can figure it out.

Worth a try—right?

I mean it ain't my style, baby, t'jap on some deal like that, but she-it. I ain't up for this big politicko t'night, an he ain't up a-tall! Gee-zuz, he don't want none a me, jes come here t'sleep. An he sure gettin his money's worth outa that.

So, what I do, I go t'crawl in with him on the side away from the door where it's more dark. Pull back the covers, slow an careful, an guess what. No room. Belly's layin over here by the side a him an they ain't no room for nobody else.

Go on around the other side a the bed an slip in there. An I'm jes layin there restin, thinkin over that mothah out there in the other room.

How he got hiseff so lost an gone in that Hongkong coat an things, an all that big word bullshid. One big mess a noise an crap—that's where he's at.

Was like that three year ago, too, but I useda daydream when I met up with him the nex time, we'd make it okay—cross over the crap in our heads an make it.

But she-it! I ain't gonna let myseff get all wound up on *his* troubles. Got troubles a my *own*. Got trouble hangin onta my own seff. Yeah.

You expectin one thing an somethin else come up, cuts the ground out from unner you—right? Gotta jump around, find youseff a new like piece a ground, somethin steady unnerneath.

Is what happen t'me—twice. Once when they shut down Madam's ole place, an the other time when I come t'that mothahfuggin Fish Pond. An I still ain't found me no good ground *there*, baby.

Else I wouldn't be layin here—right? Wonderin what t'do. With that sumbitch in the other room busy pushin me on his sleepin friend, like tryin t'*use* me.

Or whatever he's tryin. I don't know. But somethin's up here. Don't take no meddle telepathy t'figure that out. That messinger's jes too goddam gone on puttin me in bed with this distingwish sleeper.

But I ain't gonna let that bug me. I got enough ground-movin troubles without workin up any sweat over that. Put in jail, an about the time I settle down in there, they put me out again. Went t'the Paradize—never did settle down there—an then out t'the headquarters, an we's still jes settin up out there, really. An now the Fish Pond an this scene with these two.

Hang onta myseff pretty good, mosta time. Sorta make it up while I'm goin along. I mean, baby, it's a white world up front—right? Jes's white as a ghost.

Can fill you fulla hate clear up t'the top, an I mean you gotta be quick an light t'keep makin youseff up in all that ghosty white. I seen a lotta people so fulla hate all they wanna do is bust up *ever*thin.

Don't wanna get like that. You can go outa you mind tryin t'fight it *all*. An I was jes about there, too, when Hap come along.

Playin his guitar. Yeah, one night I was jes floppin around in the Paradize Hotel, soakin up booze an sneakin a weed now an then, an feelin pretty goddam high on hate, an this white sumbitch come walkin in carryin a guitar an he set down near the door an started playin an singin.

Sed t'myseff, Humph, nother one a them college-boy folksingers. Picked up my drink an went over an stood by, jes waitin for a cause t'grab that thing an bust it over his pretty blond head.

From the South. Can tell by the aksent.

But he seen me comin, read my mind. Turned on me an started playin an singin, went from one song to another like he was talkin 'em at me, an pretty soon I was so took up lissenin, I forgot all about my hate.

Started askin him t'play this an that, an he played ever one. Pretty soon the whole place's around, but he kep right on a-playin an singin straight t'me.

Tole me he could see I had the need.

An later on, I tole him how sick up t'the top with hate I was, and he put me on his lap, hung that guitar round boff us an put it a-gin my belly an started plink-plank-plunkin away, tole me t'feel it in my belly. Sed evertime he feels scattered all over hell's haff-aker an goes hateful an mad, he sets his guitar on his belly an plays, fetch some soul back.

Humph! Maybe I oughta buy Jay See a guitar. Get him t'gather up hiseff, huh.

No. Fraid not.

Gee-zuz, he wouldn't take that guitar if I was t'run right out an buy it! Too fuggin far gone lost.

An right about here, layin there goin over this in my head, is when the phone call came in. Dingaling, an he answers it, an he say—like this—he say, For YOU, Kitten. Tryin t'act smart.

Roll outa bed an pitterpatter in, take it up. It's the man from the club, wanna know if everthin's okay.

I don't tell him nothin, jes say, Oh yeah, okay.

Pretty good party?

Ummm, not so bad.

Say, Any trouble?

Oh nooo!

Then he say, if somebody lookin for another date at this party, Sharmain'll come right out, knows how t'get here.

That goddam Sharmain! Kee-ryess!

I tell the man, no I don't need no help from no goddam 'gyptian belly dancer. Tell him I got . . . ummm, like one more *dance* t'do, an then I'm goin home.

He say, Well Geegee, make it good, cause we found out you got a very importint gentlemin, practickly runs the whole coundy.

Big deal!

Okay, we hang up.

Turn around an here's Jay See, all leaned over on some magazine fulla girlie pitchers. Set down on the sofa side a him an I'm lookin too—all of a sudden he turns on me, say, Where'd you get this?

*Me* get it! Gee-zuz! It ain't *mine!*

An he shakes his head, jes shakes his head for a time, then he toss that book on the floor. Stands up an he bears down on me, wants t'know all about that phone call. *How* the man get this number? *Why's* he callin up?

I don't tell him how nothin. Was all set t'tell him I don't know nothin about no magazine—an on that phone call, that's *my* bizness. But jes's I'm about t'spit all this out, I hit on somethin else.

I tell him the man say if I ain't outa here in ten minits, they's comin in t'find out what's the trouble.

Hey, you shoulda seen that little story take ahold. I mean he ain't *sure* I'm lyin, fraid maybe somebody *is* comin. I can read it all in his face.

Can hardly keep from laughin, but I play it for all it's worth. La-dee-dah over an pick up my dress the club give me, hold it up an start pattin it down like he done his top-coat.

Say, Look what you done t'my dress! An then I take off around the room, gonna gather up the rest a my stuff.

Can't find 'em, roamin around huntin, tryin t'use this phone call for a way out.

An if I coulda found everthin easy, I might a made it before that sumbitch caught on. But I didn't.

No, cause he turn goon on me nex minit, clap a hand on the back a my neck an he say, You get in that bedroom this instint, get in there an sell you sex, or I'll deman' ever dollah I gave you *back!*

But— That's me.

No buts! An if you only got ten minits, you better be quick about it.

Is what the bastid say, pushin me along by the neck.

Well baby, number one, I'm tired, really pissed-out tired. An number two, the way things was, I figured it'd be better not t'fight 'em, lot easier t'go on in an take care a that big shot. Specially after when the man sed—importint gentlemin, runs the coundy, an all.

So I jes drop my stuff an go. I mean, he *shoves* me an I go.

It happened just I thought. Precisely as I had anticipated that it might.

It's the honest truth that some people are *born* with criminal instincts. I know all about those softheaded sociologists who have opined to the contrary; I suspect their problem is that they lack firsthand experience with the type.

Don't misunderstand me, I do respect the properly educated, certified scientist. I'm not one to disregard authority, any authority. Which is legal, etc., but what I'm trying to convey here is that I do believe some sociologists go somewhat astray sometimes, especially when confronting criminal types. And my firsthand experience with Kitten bears me out.

For example, I finally get her into the bedroom where I assumed (and here, I fear, I assumed much too much) she would uphold her end of our agreement and do what she was brought here and paid an exorbitant sum to do—namely, see to the board head's sexual pleasure—when the phone rang.

Thereby commenced what I'm driving at—her innate sense of cheating, her instinctive dishonesty.

And race has nothing to do with it! It's just that some people don't share our sense of a binding agreement. To help you grasp my point, here's a parallel: How can the world court, which some Leftists advocate America bow to, judge things fairly when it may be centuries before the common law of Ghana, for instance, approaches that of, say, Indiana!

But I tend to stray off course. What happened was this: the phone rang, and it was for her. Some man, I don't have the least idea who, nor how he got this number. Naturally this surprises me, and gives me pause. I am, after all, responsible for the Chairman's safety, as well as for protecting him against any attempts to tarnish his sterling reputation.

However, I called her to the phone and she came padding out of the bedroom, naked of course. And while she was on the phone, I stuck my head into the bedroom for a quick check.

Well, several matters emerged. First of all, right there on the dresser was this certain magazine. It . . .

But no, no, I refuse to play the role of censor. Censorship is absolutely and totally wrong. It's just as Dad said—no matter how you try to cut it, it's wrong. Last summer, up at our mountain retreat while this higher-up from N.B.C. was visiting—he and Dad are old college buddies, and they were sitting on the porch one evening, feet up on the railing, puffing after-dinner cigars, that sort of thing, and chatting about various aspects of the communist menace, when the subject came up. And it was Dad who made the very incisive observation that the only way to stop this storm of pornography which presently floods our land, threatens our children and the unintelligent, is to *ignore* it, and thereby stop advertising it. But not to censor it, because by the very *act* of censorship, you *advertise* it and thus defeat your purpose.

Therefore, rather than being prudish about this matter, what is needed is responsibility—i.e., by those in control of the nation's press and airways, who are of course our thought-leaders.

So, taking my cue from this, I'll simply not mention it. Instead, I'll ignore it like it never happened and move on to the second matter: that phone call.

It's not that I wanted to know *who* had called her. *That,* of course, was *her* business. But I did feel that, since Mr. Pennypacker was paying, we had a right to know *why* she had been called, and also *how* this whoever-it-was had learned this number. Because, why in the world would she tell anyone where she was going? Assuming she knew herself, which she didn't—she didn't know where I was *taking* her until I *got* her here, for I had steadfastly declined to divulge this.

Therefore, I interrogated her on this matter. To which her only reply was that she had to *leave!* In ten minutes! She even dropped the very clever hint that if she weren't out of this room in ten minutes, some underworld friends of hers would break into this room, or something.

At which point, I tried to reason with her. And that, of course, was a mistake. I tried to point out that she had not yet discharged her obligation, and I tried to suggest into the cavity of her hollow skull the fact that Mr. Pennypacker—although I of course didn't use his *real* name—that she had been hired by an extremely prominent individual, and so it certainly behooved her to fulfill her obligation, to live up to her end of the deal—if for no other reason than the fact of the gentleman's prominence.

All this, however, failed to sink in, I fear. Because, finally, I was forced to simply order her back into the bedroom, because, you see, she was actually in the process of getting dressed to leave, having apparently gotten this idiotic idea that since she now had a pocketbook full of money in advance, she was no longer obligated to perform the function she had been paid, in advance, to perform.

Not that I was at all surprised that she would try to wheedle out of the deal, for that seems to be her *modus operandi.* That's just what she tried to pull on me, three years ago. In reverse, so to speak. That is, she invited me to her home—not as a paying customer, but as a guest—and then she turned right around and charged me! Not only charged me, but stole all the money I happened to have been carrying—stole it.

So, in view of that experience, I was other than overwhelmed by her attempt to renege and amply able to cope with the situation.

Which brings us to the third matter. She had been, as mentioned, in there with the Chairman when the phone rang, so one would naturally assume that she had at least *begun* to fulfill her end.

I should *live* so long!—that I could make such an assumption!

Because what she had done in there all that time before the phone rang is still a mystery to me. Because Mr. Pennypacker, I had discovered during my quick check, was still asleep! He had moved not one iota from his original position, and was still right where he had been when we first entered this family suite, which was . . . well, some time ago.

I hence saw to it that she woke him up, and that was that. I left them alone together, walked quietly out the door, listening to the board head's expressions of delight and pleasure, for he did indeed have feeling for her—albeit sexual, but feeling none the less, and he is an affectionate man—I mean, *was*—and he did treat her with the utmost courtesy and kindness, much more than she deserved. But that was his usual way of doing things—he was that sort of man, above racial prejudice, the very personification of justice.

However, this time when I adjourned to the living room, I had the good sense to keep one ear cocked. And to turn down the volume of the music so that I could distinctly hear the sounds which were coming from that bedroom.

Of course there's no need for me to add to American sex literature by going into what was going on in that bedroom. Already there's been so much of that, that it's caused sex to lose its scarcity value, and what is really needed, as I mentioned earlier, is to ignore it. So I'll not nauseate you, Dear Reader, with the lurid details—the only reason I even *mention* these sounds is because they are important integral parts of my factual account.

Which is not to say that I am, ordinarily, an eavesdropper. This situation, however, was, you'll have to admit, far out of the ordinary.

So I felt it my duty to listen: bed creakings of various lengths and loudnesses, and now and then a snatch or so of dialogue—these busy sounds against the background of those symphonically-rendered folk songs from around the world, coming in softly over the piped-in hi-fi system my frat brother has installed in his motel. In certain special rooms.

And everything seemed to be going just fine, until—

All of a sudden, all sound ceased! And for quite a few seconds there was nothing—no sounds at all from the bedroom. Which, at the moment, didn't worry me, this period of silence. But then—*then*, Dear Reader, *Gad!* The beginning of the *end!*

First, this peculiar, muffled sound out of Kitten, sort of a yelping which came out sounding something like, "Ged effeggin oudder . . ." Or something equally incomprehensible, accompanied by more of her repetitious and redundant unquotable obscenities and profanities.

Well, I leapt to my feet and rushed in and found, in the dim light, nothing, apparently. I mean apparently nothing out of order.

But on second inspection realized that something must

be amiss, for only one of them was present, it appeared. Namely, the only one I found was Herman. Prone on his stomach on the bed. Kitten, who was making all the noise, appeared to be absent.

Which of course she wasn't. She was blubbering for me to *do* something, trying to tell me that something had gone wrong.

Well, that was obvious! Indeed, something *had* gone wrong—terribly, terribly wrong. Because the Chairman, it turned out, had, at this very inappropriate time, suffered a most disconcerting indisposition.

It took me a moment to realize this, but I soon saw that there could be no other rational explanation, and he did, as everyone around here knows very well, have a troublesome heart. Now here he was, lying motionless, his kingsized bulk inert.

Follows me in an he say, Why's Mister Pennypacker still sound asleep?

I say, Gee! Musta fell back t'sleep when I went for the phone, huh.

I get a nasty look outa that, so I say, Hey baby, you sure this distingwish friend wanna—*buy my sex?*

Tells me t'get in bed and wake him up an *ply my trade.* Says it like he got his lips stuck on his teeth.

I tell him he can go outside inta that other room now, an he can ply *his* trade.

He don't catch it, jes stands there waitin. Okay, I hop

in bed again, an I start singin out—Hey Mister Pennypacker, yoo hoo. Wake up, Mister Pennypacker.

Then Jay See come over and shake the mothah. Bed rocks like crazy. I mean, baby, this big blueberry hill almost too much for this bed, seem like he gonna go right through an land on the floor. An wow, what a dent he puts in the middle a this bed! Like I can hardly stay up on my side, can hardly keep from rollin down in the valley, way he's rockin this bed.

Anyhow, distingwish finally makes it. Starts chewin his teeth, snorts an gurgles, starts comin to.

Then he say, Hey Mister Pennypacker, here's Kitten. You sed you'd try her out, so here she is.

Pennypacker can't talk yet. Ain't all the way awake. Jes layin there snortin, makin them noises like he jes wanna be left alone t'sleep.

So me, I hop outa bed an I say, Well looks like I better go. He sure don't want no parts a me.

An I'm on my trilly-ass way after my clothes again.

But he comes around that bed flyin after me, grabs me an drags me back. I keep on tryin t'tell the dum mothah this dollah-whoppin Pennypacker don't want no parts a me, all he wanna do is sleep.

But he ain't havin none of it. Gee-zuz, he drags me back an throws me on the bed, an I mean, baby, by this time that distingwish can't help but be woke up.

Rolls over an he say, Hmmm, my my, what time is it?

Messinger checks his watch, say Quarder past four.

Dear dear, I didn't mean t'sleep so late!

Look who's here, Mister Pee.

Ah yes, the Negress, eh.

Well baby, I coulda sed a whole lot back on that. But for once in my stupid life I keep my big mouth shut. I mean, like now I got *two* of 'em on my hands.

So I slip unner them covers, again, an I make up cozy with this great big distingwish pennypackin piggy bank. Smile big, like the worl's bigges' tourist attrackshun, an I say—like this—I say, *Hyeee!*

You oughta hear the way I say that—coulda pass for a debutaunt.

Anyhow, this distingwish sits up an he looks down on me, an he say—I'm layin there snug in a pilla tryin t'look like a Playboy Bunny—an he say, Well well well, James say you the best piece he ever had!

Ha!

Right here's where that messinger makes tracks for the other room.

An then this distingwish say, Yeah he tell me I oughta *try* you. Goes on talkin like this, says he took haff a sleepin pill so he'd be real well rested an could find out what James ravin about back in the Fish Pond.

She-it. That sumbitch talkin about *my* trade!

Anyhow, he wants a little time t'get woke up, an then he wants me t'get outa bed an walk around—like, he wanna look me over.

We make it past that bit okay. I go paradin around in my birfday suit an he lay there lookin over his big ole belly at me, smilin this real silly-ass grin. I go through a few bumps an grinds, turn around an shake some blackass in his face.

Then I hop back in bed beside this great big mountain of a mothahfug, an I get down t'bizness. An bizness, on this distingwish, is *down*, baby, *really* down. Gotta travel down his belly t'find his bizness, an once I got it found, *it's* down. Yeah, jes a-layin there on the south side a his big hump limp's a dead chicken neck.

Kee-ryess! I thought all that prancin around I done'd raise him, jes a little. But no. Gotta start in from scratch an raise that thing myseff.

Gee-zuz, by the time that thing's up, I'm near wornout.

Wow, what a couple tricks I pull t'night, huh. That pimpin messinger, an now this ole distingwish bored head's all dried up.

You spose maybe he so busy bein a big shot he got mixed up on what that little thing a his is for?

Anyhow, I raise him, finally. Not real good, but okay. Long's I keep after it, it stays okay, but it sure feel like it's gonna die if I don't stay with it.

Then this big daddy starts makin noises like he's alive! Yeah, he gets a motion goin, first sign a life I had outa him yet. Gets a motion goin, sets this bed t'squeakin an groanin, an Kee-ryess! I mean, baby, this two ton rockin that bed puts out noises like a weepin willow in a wind storm.

So I go t'work hard now. Got everthin goin I know how t'make go, tryin everthin I can t'put some life back in this big daddy's dingus.

Then, I'm about ready t'give it up an tell him he got a dry well, an see if maybe I can talk him inta some other time —about ready t'try this when that two ton mothahfuggah gets hiseff a distingwish idea.

He say, You lay down now, an I'll get on top.

Well, baby, I could hardly believe my *ears! Him*—get on *top?*

Talk about the H bomb! Kee-ryess, anybody thinks the H bomb's a frightful pitcher oughta pitcher layin on the bottom unnerneath a *this!*

I try t'talk him outa this frightful setup, I come up—jes t'talk t'this mothah you gotta sit clear up so's you can see over his belly. Come up, an I say—like I'm still playin my debutaunt bit—say, Aw Honey! Doesn't what I'm doing make you feel *good?*

An I smile Playboy Bunny, an then I say, Wait a minit, *I'll* get on top of *you!* Ride the pony. How'd you like that, huh?

But how he'd like that never made it, cause nex thing I know this big dollah-whopper got me in his paws an he's puttin me down an rollin over on top a me, an before I got a chance t'say *no no you's too big!*—here goes me, back in my usual baddle stashun.

Nothin left t'do but say, Okay big boy, climb aboard!

Cause, I mean, baby, really, he goddam well already *is!* Sweet singin harps in heaven, he come down on me like a bag a wet rags. Covers me from asshole t'apetite! Why baby, I'm way down in some wee tiny dip in the bed—that's me, jes a deep hole in the middle a the bed. An him, here's him, that sumbitch is all over this bed—head's way up there a-gin the wall an I'm sure his feet's hangin over the other end. My butt musta been about one small inch from the floor.

Open my mouth t'talk an all I get is a mouthful a the fur on his chest. All I was gonna do was help him t'find the right home, but they ain't no helpin nohow, now, an they ain't no talkin with all that hair in my mouth.

Anyhow, he finds hiseff a home, still ain't sure which

one. I mean I was like dead unnerneath there, baby—dead. Temporary outa this world. About all I done is lay there an hope I make it up some day with all my parts in workin order.

*Phew!*

Then he starts shovin, an evertime he give a shove, I give an *offf!* Come out soundin jes like that butt-grabber I put the elbow to back in the club. *Offf!*

Meantime, this ole distingwish, he's workin up some steam. Yeah, right now he starts goin like he means it, an like maybe he gonna make it after all.

An down here, baby, I ain't sure what he means t'make. Chuggin away like a choo-choo train, I ain't sure what the hell he's meanin t'do—screw me or squash me.

So here we go—here's him, he's goin, *Ugh! Ugh! Ugh!* An here's me, I'm goin, *Offf! Offf! Offf!* An here we go in two-part harmony, *Ugh-offf! Ugh-offf! Ugh-offf!*

Then, jes when this big ole bored head distingwish's ughin and gruntin an squashin away on me like he gonna grind my ass t'hamberg, he let go this one great loud mothahfuggin grunt an same time he turn loose some real long *Ahugh* sound. Like somebody scorch his ass an he's about t'shoot through the head a the bed!

Yeah, but steada shootin off, this fat cat squash down on me once again so hard I'm sure I ain't gonna live t'tell the tale.

But I do. I make it. Oh yeah, *I* do.

But, you know what? He *don't!* No!

Give this one last squash an then he jes go, *Pheeew!* Like somebody stuck a pin in his balloon an let out all his big prideful air with a great big hiss an a rumble.

An that rumble, baby, that's the last word outa him. He gives off that, an no more. Nothin. After that, not a sound, not a move.

I lay there a minit, an then I say, Hey Lover, you done? Say, You done on me, how about rollin off, huh?

She-it! I'm only talkin inta his fur. His ears a good way off from where I'm at. Way up there on his head, an like I tole you, his head's way t'hell an gone up there. Where I'm at—shiverin shitfits! He might jes's well not have no head a-tall!

But I keep a-tryin. Say, Hey genril, roll offa me now, come on. An I start squirmin around, tryin t'get myseff out from unner. An here goes me, squashed flatter'n a fuggin pancake, wrigglin an squirmin an singin out—right inta his fur— Yoo hoo! Hey there boss, you hear me, boss? Get yer everlovin two ton offa me, will ya, yer honor sir, huh? Come on, for Kee-ryess sake, get the fug up!

Still he don't make a motion, not number one move does he make.

Nothin left for me t'do but holler out an try t'rouse that mothah in the other room. An before I can do this, I gotta put up an awful squirmin, get my face turned sidewise an lift some a that blubber enough so's I got a little peep a the outside world. An then I give a yell. Boy, I give a yell like they oughta hear it way down in city hall. An I keep up this yellin too, till that mothahfuggin messinger finds me.

Here he come on the run, in the bedroom lookin all around like maybe he thinks I'm hidin in a dresser drawer. Then he digs it, at last! An I tell him t'get me the hell out from unner here. Don't argue, jes roll you distingwish friend offa me, you sumbitch, or I'll wake 'em up in city hall.

Well baby, he hauls on that two ton, gets him offa me, an I lay there awhile tryin t'catch my breath an testin out t'see if I'm still all here.

Then I say, Hey you dum she-it, what's the matter with this distingwish? He bust a mainspring or somethin?

Jes a-layin there, right where he rolled, ain't made a move.

Jay See say, He musta pass out!

I take one good close look at that mothah's eyes, the distingwish, an I say, *Yeah*, out, *way* out!

Musta been from drinkin too much, huh. That's the messinger.

Me, I say, Oh yeah, sure, uh huh, drinkin. I say, Baby this daddy was not drinkin, he was on top a me, jazzin! No, he did *not* pass out from drinkin.

Then he say, Well then, what happen? An he say, Oh *I* know what's the trouble—heart attack!

An he zooms over t'the closit an pulls out the bored head's clothes, comes up with a little bottle a pills. Runs out the door, goes t'the baffroom, come back with a glass a water.

Sittin on the side a the bed holdin this water in one hand an the pills in the other, right unner this distingwish nose, waitin t'feed 'em.

But this daddy don't come to t'get fed. He don't come to *now*, an he don't come to *later*. I mean, baby, he's doin nothin but layin there stone-still an fish eye. Still ain't made motion number one, an by now I ain't sure he's ever gonna make a motion. Mouth open, tongue layin there in a crazy way. I lean over an take another deep look inta them wide-open fish eyes, pat him on the cheek an call his name. Jay See on the other side pattin that cheek. An baby, the only thing goin on is his head's rollin back an forth an his tongue's floppin a little—but that's the sum cottinpickin total. Nothin else.

Then he say, Good *lord,* Kitten! What did you *do?*

*Do!* I say, Baby what I done is, I got *squashed,* that's what *I* done. An I say, Jimmy boy, you wanna know somethin?

She-it, he already knows. Plain's the nose on his face! But I say it, Say, *I* do believe you bored head's *dead!*

No! Impossible! Oh God no! Is what he say.

Oh yeah, he's dead.

Stop that kinda talk, he is *not!*

He is *too,* goddam it.

He jes pass out, pass out—heart attack. Be alright in a minit, jes wait an see.

I say, Boy if I was you, I wouldn't hold my breath waitin.

Then he leans over that big distingwish belly an he gives a lissen, puts an ear a-gin the man's heart. An then, baby, his face goes whiter'n a K.K.K. sheet, an he say, Oh nooo-ooo!

Straighten up again, an guess what—he comes on mad with *me!* With me! Say, Kitten you'll *pay* for this!

*Me—pay!*

Kee-ryess! I say, Whatd'ya mean, *I'll pay.* You flippin your lid or somethin? You outa you ofay mind? This ole man jes *died,* didn't take no help from *me.* He did it *all* on his very fuggin *own.* All *I* done was get *squashed!* Gee-zuz! How many times I gotta tell you that.

Goes wanderin around the bedroom for a time, an then he's out the door an inta the other room, leavin me here alone with that corps.

I hop out an follow him in.

Settin over there in his first chair lookin like somebody jes stole his last dime. So I flop down in my chair, an here we go, back t'start, jes a-settin there, him starin at the floor an me starin at him, an that mothahfuggin ofay music havin all the say-so.

The Chairman was in a perfectly wretched state. He seemed unable to move. Matter of fact, there can be little doubt about this, for I was forced to roll him over in order to release Kitten.

And it wasn't until a moment or so later—after I'd given him his heart pill and he'd taken a glass of water with it—that his condition improved. It did, admittedly, improve gradually. But there is absolutely no basis in all honest truth to some fairy tale that's been echoing down the courthouse corridors to the effect that the board head met his end in congress with a colored whore, and I don't know how such a story could have gotten started. It is, plainly, straight out of some psychotic's sick imagination and, fortunately, it's so incredible that no one in his right mind could believe it. However, as long as it is circulating—albeit, as a joke, I suppose—I feel it incumbent upon me to render the actual facts and set you straight by presenting exactly what did happen that night.

Which was this: that Mr. P. recovered. Nevertheless, it was some time before his recovery was complete enough to talk, and even more time before he felt up to movement. Obviously, he had suffered a rather severe attack, and I was, as you might well understand, frantic with concern.

Of course this attack wasn't *my* fault. I believe I've set you straight on that already. But just for the record, let me add that Mr. Pennypacker's physician, Dr. Makepeace, has pointed out that his condition was such that such an attack might have occurred at *any* time. It's just that I happened to have *been* there when it *did* occur. In the next room, unfortunately.

Well, I did everything I could to make him comfortable and ease his condition. I strongly urged him to instruct me to call Dr. Makepeace and have him come out immediately, right to the motel. But the board head wouldn't hear of this. He flatly refused! Told me that even though he trusted the good doctor like a brother, *others* might get wind of what had happened and—even though Dr. Makepeace would never breathe a word of it to a living soul—there was a distinct possibility of scandal. Because of these others who might hear of it.

So, instead of calling the doctor, as I strongly urged,

the Chairman said he would simply rest awhile and later, after taking another heart pill, he would be ready to travel. That is, he'd be ready for the drive home—a rather far distance from this motel, since his residence is in Tanglewood-by-the-Lake. Which, in case you're unfamiliar with our area, is a suburb all the way over on the other side of the City.

In addition to which, it was already morning. Dawn had risen. It was light outside. It was, in fact, pushing 5 A.M. And when I looked out the window and saw daylight, I saw something else, too. It was, I must add, fortunate that I did see this other, for although I have no idea who he was, he certainly had no business being where he was, when he was. It was a young man, a rather faggotty-looking character in a Volkswagen, asleep. Parked right in front of this motel room.

Well, of course I had never seen either he or his car before, didn't have the slightest idea who in the world he was, nor what he wanted. I never saw him before in my life, but one thing was obvious: if he was a guest of this motel, he'd be in his room. Ergo, I quite naturally surmised that he had no business here, and I still cling to the sneaking suspicion that he was, perhaps, *tailing* the Chairman and myself. For who-knows-*what* political enemies.

Which, incidentally, is another reason why I'm so anxious that we get all the facts straight on exactly what happened that night. Because, as you can well understand, due to Mr. Pennypacker's prominence, there's no telling who it might have been, nor what sordid story he might try to cook up. To smear the good name of the late Mr. P. Because people in politics always have enemies, locally as well as on the international level, and slander is the constant threat. One must learn to sort the fact from the fiction, and gain an ability to tell which accounts are truly beneficial and which only benefit the enemy.

But, getting back to the matter of moment, I got on the phone immediately and called the desk. I asked, first, if John Cloud was there (my frat brother, the owner of the motel) and when told he wasn't, informed the desk clerk, whose name happens to be Abel Zitch, a good friend of mine whom I tip well. I said, "Abe, there's a blue Volks parked right outside my room with what appears to be an unpaid guest in it."

Whereupon that little matter was taken care of. Abe came out and in less time than it takes to tell, removed the imposter.

Kitten, meanwhile, suddenly got this frantic urge toward uncharacteristic feminine modesty. She'd been sitting slumped down in an easy chair, nude of course, and seemingly not the least bit self-conscious about it—which, I suppose, is understandable, in view of the means she has chosen to earn her livelihood. Then she leaped out of that chair and went dashing about the room, gathering up her garments. Because, you see, she had, when she went through that stripping business you'll recall my having mentioned, flung her clothing hither and thither about the suite's sitting room. Indeed, she made quite a spectacle of herself.

In response to which I felt obliged to restrain her. For she was, it seemed, in the process of making a hasty departure, a departure which, because at that time the Chairman had not recovered enough to be . . . out of the woods, so to speak, I felt duty bound to keep her right here. At least until we were certain of the eminent Mr. Pennypacker's full recovery.

Please understand my position, Dear Reader. *If* the Chairman had *not* recovered, what then? I mean, had the board head actually expired from that attack, and had I then permitted her to simply *leave,* think of the predicament *I* would have been in! Of course I would have notified the proper authorities—naturally—and when they arrived, there I'd have been, alone with the dead board head. Rest his soul.

Because, you see, the scandal would have been earth-shaking! And nation-wide! And I'd have been in one glorious pickle of a mess trying to explain it, and trying also to locate that vile little Negress whore, alias Kitten, alias Gigi Abercrombie, alias God-only-knows. For she's not *that* stupid. She would certainly have *tried* to evade the law.

So I hope you'll understand when I tell you that . . .

But let's take this step by step. She did, as mentioned, get this sudden urge toward modesty and went rushing around picking up the clothing she had scattered, as mentioned, and was about to make a hasty departure. Consequently, I was forced to be, perhaps, a mite firm. Ergo, I was finally compelled to restrain her bodily, by force, until I could get her quieted down so that I could reason with her and convince her that it greatly behooved her to remain right where she was, until the outcome of the Chairman's untimely seizure was a certainty. Because she appeared, for a moment or two, to be downright hysterical. She did, in fact, utter several loud shrieks. Said shrieks occurring at the very same time Abe was right outside our room rousing that unpaid guest, or whatever he was. And even though Abe knows the score, and was Hip to the fact that the board head and I were with another party in this suite, I felt obliged to turn down her volume a bit by holding a hand over her screaming mouth.

Which is—I might as well add right here for the benefit of certain Hook Courtians—the explanation behind what was . . . shall we say, a curiosity around the Courthouse the following Monday: namely, teeth marks in my right hand, between the thumb and forefinger.

However, we'll pass over that, for it's not really important. What is important here is the fact that the board head did—albeit, gradually—recover from his temporary indisposition. Perhaps it was her yelps, loud and in the key of high C, which helped bring him around—who knows?

But she did, finally, decide to stay with me—give her credit for that. She eventually saw that her duty was clearly to help me see this County's leading politician through the ordeal of his untimely attack, and see it through to the end.

Settin over there moanin an groanin. Goes, Oh god —*no!* Oh my god! The bored head expire! Dead! What am I gonna do now? Oh god god god!

Bored head kickin off took the starch outa this messinger. Ain't settin straight up in that chair no more. Slumpin bent over with his head in his hands.

Ain't gonna do no good jes settin there moanin an groanin. Me, I got a little itch in my right eye an I'm busy rubbin it, nex thing I know, he's lookin at me real hard, an he say, You *realize?* The bored head expire!

Kee-ryess!

I say, She-it! Baby he did not expire, he mis-*fire!* Didn't come a-tall, the bored head. Steada comin, he went!

Straightens his back an looks at me like I jes tole him he's goin blind.

I say, No big thing, baby. All you gotta do is get on that phone, call somebody t'come get the corps. Somebody dies, don't you Decent people turn him over to a funril direckter?

Then he looks at me with the saddest eyes I seen in a long long time, an he say—like I'm afraid he gonna bust out bawlin any minit—he say, Kitten you don't unnerstand!

*Yeah* baby, *what* don't I unnerstand.

I can't *do* that!

Kee-ryess baby, why not?

Be-*cause*—of the *scandal!*

Scandal? What scandal? I tell him wasn't nobody's fault, that distingwish jes died, that's all. Gee-zuz! What scandal?

Say, Kitten we'd boff be *Imp*licaded! Don't you *see?* They'd send you t'*jail,* it'd be in every paper in the country!

Well, baby, I don't go this crap, sendin me t'jail. Sounds like he's tryin t'con me inta somethin here. I mean, how the fug m'I gonna go t'jail—they think I killed the mothah with my twoit?

But I hold my big satch shut an let him keep on his speel. Say, You'd go t'*jail,* Kitten, an *me,* this would be a black mark against *me* for the rest a my *life!*

Black mark! Hey I coulda tole him somethin about black marks. Yeah! Oh yeah! Black marks an jails.

Then he puts his head back in his hands an carries on with more a this moanin an groanin.

Way he's behavin recall t'me what Hap always sayin about horin. Say, it's a lot easier for a girl t'peddle her pussy than it is for a man t'peddle his mind.

I don't argue with him when he say that, but I ain't sure he knows what he's talkin about. I mean, I never had t'peddle my mind, but he ain't no woman so he never had t'peddle his pussy.

But watchin this mothah goin through all this moanin an groanin an head holdin steada gettin on that phone an doin somethin, I don't know, maybe Hap got a point.

Anyhow, too bad for him, is all I can say. Me, I gotta split.

So I pitterpatter over an grab my pocketbook, figure I'll get my blouse and leatards out, put them on, put my heels on, jam everthin else in that pocketbook an take off.

Oh yeah! That's what *I* think!

But that rough tough lily-white mothah, he don't see it my way. No.

Cause I come outa the bedroom from fetchin my pocketbook, he's standin over lookin out the front winda. I don't pay no mind t'that, jes go round huntin up my clothes. Grab my bra an put that on. Money's in there good an safe.

Find my pants—guess where. On top a the tee vee's rabbit ears!

Then, I'm all set t'climb inta my leatards—whoops!—that mothahfuggin messinger grab 'em outa my hands. Yeah, I'm standin there on one foot, holdin up the other, jes about t'slip a leg down, *Whissst!* Gone.

An nex thing I know, he's on that phone loud an nasty.

Me, like a dum burrhead cottinpatch conkubine, I's so goddam surprise, all I can do's *stand* there.

He say, That you Zitch? You not on you *toes*, boy! They's a car parked right outside this *room!* With somebody *in* it! Asleep! I thought I tole you—

I take a quick peek out the winda. They's *three* cars—Thunderbird, Cadillack, an that Voltswagon with Hap inside sleepin.

Move like I got springs on my feet, zip around there grabbin up the rest a my stuff, jam 'em stockins down in that pocketbook an I'm on my flyin way—leavin them leatards an shoes behind, zoomin over t'that door.

An guess who's waitin for me, on *this* side. Yeah, the sumbitch beats me there, drops that phone an makes it there haff a hair in front a me. Grabs me an turn me around, twist my arm up behind my back, cop style.

Say, where you think *you* goin in such a hurry?

Drags me back over t'the phone, an he say Zitch if it isn't gone in less than a minit—

Hangs up, bangs it down, cause me, baby, I'm puttin up a shout an a holler. Yeah! I'm tryin t'yell loud enough for Hap t'hear, hope he come bustin in here an get me loose.

An I might a made it, too, if that bastid didn't bang down that phone an clap a hand over my mouth—what he done. Then, like I'm squirmin an kickin an tryin t'get loose, but he got me too good, hand tight over my mouth an that arm pullin up my back, an the only thing I got left t'do is, if I can jimmy that hand loose a little off my mouth, I can sink my teeth in it. So I'm workin on this with my free hand an I get it out jes enough, an—oh yeah, I set my teeth on it—chomp down on that hand with all my might an hang on, jes a-bitin an a-chewin away.

That don't please him none. No! *He* dam near let out a holler when I come down on that hand. An then what he done was, shove me along back inta the bedroom an push me down face-first on that bed beside the dead distingwish—I'm still chewin away for all I'm worth—an he grabs a pilla an lays it over my head!

Hey, you ever been held down like that? Tell you somethin, baby, it ain't fun.

All I can do now is try for air. Gotta let up on his hand an jes try for air.

Get my head turned t'one side some, find a little air hole, an I jes lay there, do nothin else but *breathe*.

Till he lets me up, an by that time I'm haff dead. All I can do t'stagger over t'the bedroom winda, jes in time t'see the Voltswagon tail lights goin around the last bend. Some man standin there—Zitch.

Then, knock on the door, an Jay See hollers it's okay now Zitch, I'll talk t'ya later.

I'm sore tempted t'give another holler, big an loud, see if I can get that Zitch t'come back an find out. But I figure it ain't worth the chance, cause this goddam rack-iteerin messinger's in a terrible state, liable t'kill me, I don't be careful.

Standin there in the bedroom door, shakin. Kee-ryess, I can see his knees wobblin right through his pants. Comes over t'me an puts a hand on my shoulder, an that hand's goin like a motor. Say, Now Kitten you behave youseff. An he takes off tellin me how he re-*strain* me for my own *good!*

*Phew!*

Oh yeah, my own good! Gee-zuz!

She-it. I don't fight the bastid, not no more. Tell my-seff, Girl now's the time for passive rezistence.

Herk's got a big thing with passive rezistence—useda walk the pickitline. Say you can use it any time, like you run inta some kinda trouble, won't do you no good t'struggle—turn on this passive rezistence.

So! Nothin else I can count on, right now. Cause, I mean, baby, this motherin messinger's sick in his redtop head, pushin that pilla down on me like that. An he still shakin like you can't tell what he might try nex.

Okay, I don't argue. But I can't stand bein here tween his shakin an that bored head's starin, so I stumble outa that bedroom an back t'the sittin room, plop down in my chair.

Tags along an plop down in his, an here we go, settin there starin. Again. Him shakin, an me—Gee-zuz! I oughta be the one *shakin*—right?

She-it, I ain't got a good shake left in me, jes set there feelin pissed out tired.

Nobody say nothin for a long time, an then he pipes up, say, You *with* me now?

Dig *that* crap! *With* him! Feel like askin him where the fug *else* do he think I'm at, huh? But I keep it shut, an all I say is, Yeah baby, with you now.

He say, Okay cause this's *our* problem.

Oh yeah, uh hum, *our* problem.

Ain't mine, an it ain't yours, it's ours!

Oh yeah, uh hum, ours.

She-it. Fore the bored head dies, it's me me me. An now, it's we we we. *Our* problem. Big distingwish layin there, not a motion, an now *we*'s in trouble.

Okay, passive rezistence, so I jes simple-ass my way along, I say, Okay Jay See, what a *we* gonna *do* now, huh?

He say, We gotta think a somethin, think a somethin, try t'think a somethin.

She-it. Bout all I can think is, how the hell did *I* get in all this *we* mess. I *knowed* this Fish Pond thing put me in a new *class*, but I *mean!* Kee-ryess! If ole lady luck don't do me no better'n this, I'm gonna quit this gig an go right back t'the Paradize Hotel!

That's rockbottom, baby, really down, but I ain't so sure I'm gonna like it where I'm at. Paradize was rough —oh yeah—but it was never *this* bad.

I mean, if some john starts shovin you around, you always got a lotta other girls right near by, give a holler an they come a-runnin, claw the bastid bloody.

I seen it happen.

Even since they pulled that raid on us—the coundy done that, not the city—toss everbody's ass in jail, an ever since I got out it's been bad. Uphill. Went t'the Paradize —an I mean if you wanna come outa that jungle the nex mornin with a jingle in you jeans, baby, you really gotta go some. Cause they's twice's many chicks as tricks, an they got *ten* times more ways t'get you money back, that Paradize.

Like, you get lucky some night an some john pick you outa that mob a hens, go upstairs an that's five. But then, you gotta cut that five right in haff with the house, so what you got left is two an a haff—right? Okay, come back down, order somethin from the bar—anythin, it don't matter—an all you got left is *one* an a haff. Order somethin t'drink t'go with whatever you order in the first place, an then all you got left, baby, is a *haff!* One fuggin fifty cents. Hamberg's a dollah, scotch is a dollah, everthin's a mothahfuggin dollah!

Racket them Paradize people got come close t'the one them politickoes got, huh.

But I'll tell you one thing, baby—nobody *dies* on you there. Not that I ever knowed. Some trick that far gone, he ain't gonna show up in the Paradize.

Anyhow, what I'm sayin, he still over there mumblin—think a somethin, think a somethin, oh lord we jes gotta think a somethin.

I'm sittin there scratchin my head, but the only thing I can think of is, how the hell m'I gonna get my ass outa here. Alive, an with that hunner in my bra.

Not long after that disquieting incident with Kitten, I returned to the bedroom to check on the Chairman and found him propped up in bed, his massive countenance radiant with health and good fellowship.

But of course I became insistent—made him stay right there and rest. He was strongly in favor of leaving immediately, which was understandable. After all, he hadn't expected to be gone all night when he invited me out to dinner, and undoubtedly his wife was expecting him.

"But," I said, "even though I won't hear another word out of you about getting out of bed so quickly after your seizure, I must insist that you give me permission to telephone your wife and tell her where you are and that everything's all right, etc."

However, he withheld said permission and flatly refused to let me make even *this* call. His rejoinder being that he frequently takes off to overnight meetings—with the Senator, and stays all night at the Senator's house.

Which the Senator will readily bear me out on. Mr. Pennypacker has been a guest of his both at home, in our town, and at the Senator's State Capitol domicile, which was where the Senator was while all this was happening. Well, the State Capitol is over two hundred miles away, and even though there's a direct turnpike connection, such a drive is not the sort a man in his sixties would be expected to make—up and back, all in one day.

Therefore, I would have made that call to his wife, overriding his insistence that I not make it, would have made it except for the very real and central fact that he was still in rather questionable condition and I just couldn't bring myself to bestir him by doing anything against his wishes, even for his own good.

What I did do, then, was this: I managed to have breakfast sent to our rooms. It wasn't 6 A.M. yet, and the motel restaurant's policy is not to bring breakfast to your room before 8. But I put in another call to the desk and prevailed upon my friendship with Abe, and breakfast was forthcoming.

Mr. Pennypacker, it should be noted right here, had, despite his seizure, a magnificent appetite that morning. It certainly was a heartening sight to see him propped up in bed wolfing down all those pancakes, and even a sizable side order of sausage.

Henceforth, fortified by that solid breakfast, it became virtually impossible to keep him in bed. He simply would not hear of it. Climbed out on his own and marched right into the bathroom as if nothing more eventful had occurred during the night than a good sound sleep. Went to the bathroom and . . . well, he went in and showered and shaved and got fully dressed.

But he didn't leave. No, I staunchly forbade him to do that. We all remained there for quite some time—the better part of the day, in fact. But he was up and about and chipper. Came out of the bathroom and seated himself comfortably in the living room and was his grand old friendly smiling self. Talked to Kitten and I as if absolutely nothing had happened.

Which, as anyone who knew him well enough will bear me out, was his manner, his personality, his character. He was indeed that sort of man, the type who can overcome misfortune, the sort who doesn't let his own indisposition impair his relations with others.

He was, of course, concerned about his wife. Naturally. And in order to fix things with her . . . (I thoroughly dislike being compelled to tell you this, for it may seem I'm making him seem the sort of man who might be tempted to tell his wife a falsehood. Which he certainly was not!) However, he was, by now, in a bind, so to speak. And what he did was in no way a reflection on his marriage, for you must understand that it was this seizure which prevented him from going home. Albeit, late, perhaps, but home nevertheless.

What he wanted to do was avoid worrying Mrs. Pennypacker, bless her heart, and consequently he put through a call to the Senator's State Capitol home. Which call is duly noted on the motel's bill, which I have in my personal tax file. And it was received by the Senator's butler, Oswald, who relayed the message to the Senator when he arose later that morning. And the message was to call Mrs. P. and tell her that Mr. P. had passed the night in the Senator's house and he just wanted her to have this message so she wouldn't worry.

Which, as I've said, is understandable. And certainly in no way a reflection on their fine marriage, held together as it was for the best part of their lives.

Now all locally who knew him personally will clearly recall that he was quite the conversationalist, so it should come as no earth-shaking shock when I relate to you that we passed most of that Saturday in conversation. Good shoptalk about the inside workings of the County political situation, as well as how he planned to handle the matter of Welfare's proposal, and my report, at Monday's board meeting. And just for the record I might add that he did plan a very strong approach to the defeat of that $3,000 give-away scheme for the furtherance of creeping socialism—albeit, by using my report as the battering ram with which to spank, so to speak, those sob sisters in Welfare. I mention this intention in passing, and only because, the way it worked out, even though my report did prove highly effective and I'm certainly not complaining, it probably would have been used even more effectively had Mr. Chairman presided that Monday.

But wait—again I tend to leap ahead of myself. It was, instead, a day devoted to talk and rest. The morning was passed in good shoptalk, and then during the afternoon while the board head, as per my suggestion, took a nap, Kitten held forth.

I mean—don't get me wrong here—I mean she *talked.* I did make an attempt to dissuade her from turning herself into a virtual chatterbox—by suggesting that we watch TV. But she declined this (and in doing so, showed a startling degree of disregard for the public airways, I might add). Ergo, we talked, and I learned from her near-incomprehensible, jargon-laden, profane and obscene chatter that she now lives . . .

Well. I'm not sure I should even go into this.

However, just to sort of round out this account, I suppose it won't hurt. Although I'm sure that when I tell you *how* she lives, you will be as deeply shocked as I was upon hearing it. But shock, sometimes, is what we sorely need to snap us out of our lethargic indifference to the internal menace which threatens to turn our great land of freedom and opportunity into a totalitarian dictatorship.

Ergo, she lives in an actual *commune!* She didn't *call* it that, of course, but from her description, that is precisely what it is. A commune with five others, who, to judge strictly from *her* description of them, are a ghastly gang of outcasts and derelicts. Including one character who, again going strictly on what she told me, was perfectly *swish!* And another one of this weird club of oddballs had at one time, according to Kitten, been, of all things, an airline hostess!

Now I sat perfectly poker-faced while she was relating these fantastic facts of her home environment. I even pretended to be completely bored with the whole matter, just sat there cleaning my fingernails while she rambled on. By which I propose to convey to you that I had no reason to suppose she might be making it all up. On the contrary, I discovered no reason to doubt her word whatsoever—not even excluding that implausible part about the airline hostess, although how in the world a girl with enough on the ball to become an airline hostess could degenerate to a point where she'd live in a biracial commune is beyond my powers of comprehension.

Moreover, this commune exists right here and now in our very own political subdivision—which is equally beyond my comprehension—and is supported by the money Kitten obtains from the sale of her sex. This latter revelation being totally believable in view of the sort who do, obviously, live there.

Needless to say, I would liked to have put all this into my report on the unemployables. And had this talk with her occurred prior to the writing of said report, you can bet your bottom dollar it would have been included.

But over and above that aspect of unfortunate timing, I was presented (ergo, in a way she seemed totally unconscious of) with a vivid firsthand rendering of the actual facts of the communist threat from within. Apropos of this, I got the distinct impression that there are a couple of individuals there which we might class as self-styled *intellectuals*—albeit, in the worst sense of that much overused word. Because she actually told me, Dear

Reader—and the following is an accurate and direct quote—that she and these others live *un-American!*

Even now as I write this, it makes the palms of my hands sweat to think of it. Imagine—*un-American!*

It just goes to show you. I mean, we are constantly pelted by large segments of the press, with the woolly-brained liberal line to the effect that the dangers of communism are purely external, not internal. So I broach the matter of this chat with Kitten to demonstrate how deep in lethargic inaction we are, and what our utter lack of vigilance has wrought.

Oh I'm willing to grant that her immature dream of paradise is, perhaps, charming to some—misfits, loners, and losers—but it's perfectly unrealistic and, as any right-thinking individual knows very well, deceptively dangerous. Especially when you stop to realize that this gang of hers was composed of those elements from the fanatical fringe: i.e., Leftists, Beatniks, perverts, and psychopaths per se, none of whom would take a job and become useful Americans serving their employer, even if such were offered to them. For it became abundantly clear from what she said that they much prefer to be supported by prostitution and other such degradations, and devote their time and energies to eroding the American Dream.

Well, since learning of this totally incomprehensible phenomenon, I've mentioned this commune around the Courthouse. And there have been those who expressed disappointment, along with their horror, because I didn't have her taken into custody right then and there, and placed somewhere to be treated, and eventually, educated to the cancerous hate-mongering and total degeneration that communism engenders. It has been repeatedly suggested that all she needs is a little psychiatric counseling to make her able and willing to adjust to our free society, with all the benefits such an adjustment would bring her, including the pride and happiness of holding down a decent job. Because, as we all know, there must be some emotional disturbance somewhere in anyone who, driven by some mad compulsion, drifts into communism.

And ordinarily I would be the first to suggest that Kitten's difficulty is definitely emotional, and/or educational. However, at the time she was relating all this, I was so totally concerned with the Chairman's welfare that I fear I was not altogether alert—enough to take such steps for her education as have been suggested. Secondly, *her* education would have to begin exactly at the beginning. Because, you see, she's *illiterate!*

She told me so herself! Don't ask me *how* she ever managed to completely avoid even a basic education—in America!—but she did. Either that, or she is absolutely the best prevaricator I have ever encountered.

At any rate, I certainly felt ill-prepared to attempt, there and then, an explanation comprehensible to her, setting forth the irrationality of communism compared to the God-given wisdom and scientifically sound sense of our free enterprise system. Not only because of her unfortunate illiteracy, but also because it became obvious, as she discussed her present domicile, that she has been tragically duped by foreign influences. Ergo, she just would not have understood me.

But, possibly the most engrossing aspect of this entire

matter is, to me, that rather than erupting with righteous and well-founded wrath at her, personally, I was able to see clearly that she, herself, was not really to blame. No, I don't blame her, for her inability to comprehend these more sophisticated distinctions and discriminations. I lay the blame on her illiteracy—that's what has led her down the primrose path to disaster, and that's what must be remedied.

Nor, I might add, do I align myself with those who feel that because of *what* she is, she should be shipped back to Africa. For I think that the Negro, generally speaking, can take pride in his advances, even though he often seems backward by *our* standards. Because, just think, not so very long ago he was subjugated as a slave in the South, and before that, he was back in the jungle with absolutely *no* cultural advantages whatsoever!

But I stray off course again. To trim my sails a bit and get back to more essential matters, let me outline a few things I learned, as she chattered, about what a small world we live in, and how our paths do sometimes cross in mysterious ways we are, at the time, unaware of.

*Item:* When the County raided the City's red-light district as part of our clean-up on gambling and prostitution, Kitten was sent to jail. Having, at that time, not found her way out of that vile institution she was in when I first encountered her.

*Item:* When she got out of jail, instead of finding a decent, honest job, she adopted a defeatist's attitude and gradually took on a sort of Beat outlook of no-work-at-all-costs.

*Item:* This thrust her into the company of people

who, to judge by her own description, are not only the sort our County Welfare Department would coddle as so-called unemployables, but who, quite clearly, are communist oriented! By their own admission!

*Item:* Having thus chosen a life of prostitution and picked people from the underworld for companions, (*companions?—parasites* would be a better word), she must, I fear, now be classed among those who are politically and morally subversive.

In short, she is a tragic example of America's need for better education at all levels, being so completely illiterate that she is, it seems, totally unaware of her part in this conspiracy to destroy America from within. And one of these days something will have to be done about all this by we who value our Heritage, before more emotionally disturbed and under-educated individuals fall prey to this ruinous Evil, communism.

However, that's enough about my little chit-chat with Kitten. I have, I fear, led you astray from what you are surely much more urgently concerned with—namely, the board head's welfare. Which, by sundown, was well on the way to recovery. Or so it seemed, for I'm no M.D. and can't say, in any way that would hold up in court, if it ever comes to that, that he was fully and completely recuperated. But he certainly *seemed* so. Indeed, he got up from his afternoon nap, strode into the bathroom, dashed cold water in his face, came out, rubbed his huge hands together briskly, and demanded to know where dinner was.

To which I quickly responded by going to the phone and ordering dinner for three sent to our rooms immediately. Another matter, that dinner for three, which anyone who wants to can verify, from either my own tax records or the motel's. Should anyone care to go so far as to want to verify this.

Well, dinner arrived, and I must say it was a convivial affair. Mr. P. was in great form, and Kitten was not unresponsive. I, too, relaxed and enjoyed myself, having determined that since there was nothing I could do, at this time, for the tragedy her life has become, I would forget it and enter into the mood of the meal, established by the Chairman's magnetic presence.

Following which, Mr. Pennypacker announced in no uncertain terms that he would hear no more pleas about resting, that he was fully able to travel now and was forthwith departing for his home.

Which is the last I saw of him. Alive. Or, to be precise, the last time both Abel Zitch and I saw him alive, for Abe (and he'll bear me out on this) saw us all drive out of that motel—the Chairman in his Cadillac on his way to his home in Tanglewood-by-the-Lake, and Kitten and I in my Thunderbird. Of course, at one point, Abe did say he *thought* he saw the board head in the front passenger seat of the Cadillac and *me* driving—that's what he said he *thought* he saw but has since thought harder, and remembered more clearly and will readily tell anyone who is curious to know, that I was driving my *own* car and Mr. Pennypacker was at the wheel of *his* own car. And Abe will, if need be, testify to this effect in court.

I might explain here, to those unfamiliar with our political situation, that there are rumors—oh yes there are—which seem to have gotten started down in City Hall. Incomprehensible as it is to even suspect our dear City fathers of electronically eavesdropping (bugging) a motel room, *some* of them are not above *implying* some such mysterious access to information substantiating these madcap rumors. So it's most pertinent to realize that there is considerable hostility to our County government, since we override them in certain key matters dear to their dishonest pocketbooks, the crackdown on gambling and prostitution being one example. And they are a vindictive bunch, too, as witness these rumors. Which, according to one version reaching the Courthouse of late, has it that—(ridiculous, I realize, but I feel I should not refrain from mentioning it)—which has it that Mr. P., rest his soul, expired in the motel! Which, as you now certainly know full well, is absolutely and entirely without any foundation whatsoever.

But I don't wish to dwell on these fairy tales which rise like a stinking mist from the swamps of City Hall, and I know you are surely curious to find out just what did exactly happen. That is, just how Mr. Pennypacker did meet his mysterious end.

Well, I'll tell you all I can about it. But, frankly, nobody knows, beyond the shadow of a doubt, and I know nothing much more than what I've already told you. Because the last time I saw him alive was, as I've repeatedly said, when we all three left the motel. Which must have been . . . oh, seven-thirtyish or eight, something like that. At which time, we, Kitten and I, let him go. Or, more precisely, helped him out and into his car, then waved good-bye, got into my Thunderbird and followed his Cadillac through the motel's premises to the driveway onto the highway, where he turned south and we turned north. And that, in all honest truth, is virtually the last I saw of him.

Of course, hindsight is a lot better than foresight, and looking back on it, I can see what I should have done: i.e., there was this one important matter about which I was, I'll admit, remiss. Namely, I might have put off driving Kitten home immediately, and I might have followed the Chairman's Cadillac all the way out to Tanglewood-by-the-Lake and thereby made dead certain that he arrived safely. But at the time, he was so full of insistences that he was perfectly all right and able to make it on his own—and he did seem well, as I've said—and he went to such great lengths to assure me he could get home by himself that I quite simply . . . well, I just let him go. His cheeks were nicely flushed, it should be noted, and he had that cheery twinkle in his eye that we all knew so well. His step, as he went out to his car, may have been a mite unsteady, but, considering the night he'd had, was *that* any wonder?

So, anyway, for those of you who are unfamiliar with the tragedy which thereafter befell us, I'll relate, in the next chapter, how he was eventually found.

He ain't done nothin for the longes' time, jes set there in that chair holdin his head, moanin an groanin, tellin me t'think a somethin.

Think a somethin, think a somethin, oh lord we jes gotta think a somethin.

Then, like we ain't thought a nothin, he say, Might's well have breakfes. Gets on the phone an calls Zitch again, tells him t'send it over.

Pretty soon, here come breakfes, right up t'the door. Makes a wave for me t'go inta the bedroom with the dead bored head, then he opens the door for Zitch t'roll this cart in.

Three breakfeses. One for me, an one for him, an one for the dead bored head.

Okay, we eat. Me an him, not the bored head.

He picks up his tray an moves from his chair over t'my end a the room, set down in another chair with his back t'the bedroom. Say, I don't wanna *see* him.

The bored head. I say, Gonna stay jes's dead no matter which way you's lookin, Lover.

Aw shut up an try t'think a somethin.

Anyhow, we finish breakfes, an he looks like he's feelin better now. Leans back in his chair, puts his feet up on the coffee table, starts pickin his teeth. Give out a couple belches, then he lays them blue eyes on me an he say, Kitten I think you an I're stuck here for the day.

Yeah?

Yeah, I'm afraid we can't do nothin till dark.

What're we gonna do after dark?

Well that's what he don't know. That's why we gotta think a somethin.

Got all day long t'think, eh. Hummm. Okay, so we're thinkin.

Kitten—he say—I hope you realize what a dire perdicka-min we's in.

Oh yeah, baby, I realize, uh hummm, *we's* in.

Then I say, Hey I jes thought a somethin. We better put the mothah back in his clothes before he goes cold an stiff on us, less you want everbody t'know he was naked's a jaybird when he went.

An he say, Yeah that's right! Oh my God, I'm glad we thought a that.

You catch that, baby? Glad *we* thought a that.

Anyhow, we go inta the bedroom an set t'work. An when I say work, work is what I mean. Kee-ryess!

Start out with the unnerwear—gotta roll him this way an put one arm in, then roll him the other way, put the other arm in. Then comes his shorts. Gotta pull an tug an grunt—I do this part. Jimmy, he holds up one leg, an then we do the other leg, an then the trouble's jes beginnin. Yeah, cause now we gotta pull them shorts up around his ass. Roll him one way, pull up a little, roll him the other way, pull up some more.

Time we got this distingwish in his unnerwear, I'm about shot.

Settin on the edge a the bed takin a breather, an I say, Hey messinger, whatd'ya guess this very distingwish bored head weigh?

He say, Oh he knows what he weigh—everbody knows what Mister Pennypacker weighs. Weighs three hunner pounds!

Ooh-wee! Gee-zuz, that pisser sure do pack a lotta pennies, huh. That's me.

Get a bad eye back on that. Anyhow, then we set t'work again. First his shirt—an that ain't no small deal, cause we gotta get that on so good you can button him up right down the front. All the way, every fuggin button.

An then his pants. Same way we did his shorts, sep his pants's worser, cause they's tight on him t'begin with, an we gotta roll him back an forth, back an forth, tryin t'get the shirttail in. An then some more rollin, tryin t'get them zipped up an his belt buckled.

Then Jimmy goes through this bit with the tie. I near

crack up over that. He never put a tie on somebody *else,* what he say. Can tie his *own* tie okay, but *this!*

Ends up sittin up at the top a the bed holdin the distingwish head in his lap, tryin t'tie it that way. An me, I end up so weak from laughin, we gotta rest up again, fore we can go on with his coat.

Meantime, baby, this mothah's goin stiffer by the minit. I can feel it. So I say, Hey maybe we better like fold this big daddy up so when he go all the way stiff on us, he won't be so fuggin long. Maybe we can handle him better, doubled over, like.

Sets down t'think on this, an then he say, Better yet, let's see if we can put him in a chair, get him in a chair.

Yeah, that's a good idea.

I run out t'the other room an get a chair, drag it in beside the bed, an we sorta roll that big bored head offa the bed an inta this chair. It's a mess gettin him right *in* that chair, cause for a time he liked t'roll right on over an land on the floor! But Jimmy run around an kep his top part from fallin over too far an goin past the chair, an I push the bed back some, an we finally get him goin inta the chair jes right.

Some more ughin an gruntin an sweatin, an we got him up settin in that chair jes's nice's can be. Still got his eyes buggin out on you an his mouth hangin open, but what the hell, can't have everthin! He's *in* the chair.

Okay, but the bed's a wreck. Look like wild animals slep here.

Anyhow, we go back t'the other room now, an flop down again. Me in my easy chair, an him on the sofa keepin his back on the bored head.

Huff and puff awhile, an then he say, You wanna watch tee vee?

Say, Naw.

An he say, You, er, eh, um, *ever* watch tee vee?

Sure! Once in awhile. Watch them news shows.

*News!*—he say—Hummm!

Yeah, watch them news shows t'cheer for the Vee-et Cong or the Panamas, any a them people tryin t'get loose from the Pentagons.

Puts a sick look on his face. Turns away an stares at the floor awhile.

Then he say, Well let's put our mind on our perdickamin. Where in the *world* shall we *take* him?

Beats me, baby. I say, Maybe we oughta bury the mothah, dig a hole an put him in it. That way, nobody'll ever know, huh.

He say, *Yeah* but *where?*

Oh out in the country some place, *any* place.

Could take the turnpike—he say—an go way up state an take him back out in the woods. I know a place, a mountan lodge.

Okay.

But then he say, No no, it'll be *dark!* Even t'dig a grave we need *light*. Oh god, oh god!

An he's back t'that.

Then—like I take pitty or somethin—I say, Hey I got it. Let's take him out where I live. We can set up lights—got three extenshun cords an all kinda lightbulbs, can set up an dig a hole out there.

Say, Where you live, Kitten?

I say, Oh it's call the I double A double P, Internashunal Associashun for the Advancemin of Po*lite* People.

Takes the rest a the day, almost, the I double A double P. Gotta tell him all about it, keeps askin queshuns. An for a time it looks like we's gonna end up takin this chair-settin corps out there.

He wanna know where it's at, so I tell him almost the end a the thruway, way off out there, down a couple back roads an like that, an then you come t'this gate.

Got that thing wired, baby. I don't tell *him* this, but anytime you open that gate it rings a bell in the house. Jes looks like some ole farm gate goin inta some ole field, but it's wired! Chahley done that.

An I ain't tellin *no*body how we get the lectrick!

Big ole house, jes gone t'seed, till we come along. Herk was first, he was the one found it. An he tole Mary Lou an me, an we tole Hap, an like that.

But he wanna know more about how I got out there, so I tell him. Me an Mary Lou—we was workin in that cathouse—an the coundy put us in jail, an when we got out we was broke. Madam was gone, took off with her man, this ole washed-up cop from the vice squad. An Jackie was gone too, nobody knows where. Rest a us queenies from them eight places up and down the street, we was left high and dry, cause they wasn't gonna open them places up no more.

Anyhow, me an Mary Lou was hangin out in the Paradize, but so was everbody else. Big mob scene, too many girls, not enough trade. The law was tight an the johns was scared t'come. Me an Mary Lou was about ready for Sykesville, an here come this cat name Herk, an he was a friend a Mary Lou—tole her he stole this car one night an driv way out in the country an found this ole house. An he say, Come on out an live, plenty a room.

So we do. First they was jes the three of us, an then we got Hap in, an he brung along Chahley, an he brung June. Chahley was gonna study t'be a dockter but they wouldn't let him in the school. An June, she got pregnent in the airlines, had t'quit.

An Shakespeer—he's a dog—he jes happen t'drop by one day. Herk give him that name an he stayed on.

An Perry—he's a gay—June found him layin on the road one night about a week ago. Had this awful fight, some boyfriend was jealous, sumbitch beat him up an left him on the road.

Then Jay See wanna know, whatd'ya *do* out there?

An I tell him, hell that's easy, we got persuits. That's what Herk calls 'em. Like Herk, he makes up pomes. An Hap, he plays guitar an makes up tunes. An Chahley, he does the wirin an the plummin, an when he's done with that, he jes sets an watches tee vee, waits for the nuclear bomb. An June, she took a while t'get over her operashun —Chahley done that—an then she cleared out a patch an started a gardin, an now she's up of a mornin bright an early, scratchin away in that gardin. An Perry, he been doin all the cookin an housework. An me an Mary Lou, we been hangin out in the Paradize, doin the best we can there, till I got this gig. An Shakespeer, he got the best racket—all that shaggy little sumbitch do is eat an sleep, chase rabbits an squirrels.

Hey, I don't mean Shakespeer's *use*less. No, cause he can smell trouble a mile away, put up a howlin bark.

Ain't nobody useless at the headquarders, that's the good part.

Anyhow, I go on telling how we got the rules, too. Main rule is, you ain't allowed t'hinder nobody else. Like, outside the headquarders—with the Decent people—everbody jackin off somebody else, tryin t'keep off the shiddy end a the stick—right? Okay, inside, they ain't no stick, so they ain't no shiddy end.

Unamerakin, that's what Herk call how we live. Like what we got is the moneybox, sets on topa the mantle in the livinroom, an any time somebody got money he puts it in that box. That's what we buy grosseries an stuff with.

Somebody wants somethin, we hold a meetin. Everbody gotta be in favor—that's another rule Herk made up. But that ain't so hard, t'get everbody in favor, cause we go by, if it's good for the one wants it, an he's good for us, then *it's* good for us. Like Herk needs paper an typeriter ribbins, an June needs seed an gardin tools, an make-up too, cause she's always wore it, an Hap needs guitar strings, an Chahley buys medical stuff so's if somebody get sick he can fix 'em up, an me an Mary Lou an Perry, we do the grossery shoppin.

Biggest buy we ever done was when Chahley took everbody an went t'this junkyard an come off with a whole lotta pipes an winda panes, stuff like that. Made us a baffroom—Chahley, with everbody else helpin—an he even put a shower in it.

Pipes rattle like crazy, but what the hell.

An everbody brung somethin there, too. June brung a lotta clothes an me an Mary Lou wear 'em. Herk brung barbells, an him an Hap use them, down in the basemin of a mornin.

Yeah, an everbody gets along okay, too. I mean, we had us some bad spats. Gee-zuz, them first few weeks we was always haff a hair away from downright fights. Then Herk made the constitushun—rules-a-thumb, what he call 'em—an that did away with a lotta hollerin an spattin.

Tellin Jay See all this, an I can see by the looks he's layin on me he don't go what I'm sayin.

Then he say, Kitten don't you know the way you's livin is il*lee*gal?

She-it. How bout that! Kee-ryess!

I come on givin him my biggest most pickaninny look, like straight offa massa's back forty, an I say, Wha'sat you say, Huh-nay?

That puts this rough tough lily-white mothahfug on like mad, an he's fillin the room with his gas.

Me—inside my blackass skull an back behind that pickaninny, my mind's jes havin hiseff a shake an a shimmy. Illeegal! I mean, dig that mothahfuggin chickenpluckin—illeegal.

Wanna know somethin? These white folks kill me, baby. Oh yeah! They jes kill me with all this gas on *lee*gal an *ill*eegal, an all the tons a bullshid they lay on top a that.

I mean they made it a-gin they law t'do *any*thin, less it suits *them*. Like, you ain't allowed t'kill nobody—right? An then these bastids turn right around with this law where *you* gotta pay *taxes*, so's *they* can kill everbody *they* don't *like!*

An that's *lee*gal! Oh yeah, it gotta be leegal. That's why they pay them taxes, so's when you gets yours, it's leegal.

Call that Defense, baby, an it's somethin like the spit-back. Steada whiskey, they got money. Steada coke, they got Defense. Herk calls that Trick-a-nomics.

An space, too. Yeah they spit a lotta money out in space. They sweat that space somethin awful!

Anyhow, mosta them white mothahs ain't really livin. She-it, they jes movin through it dead t'the world. Like rain water down the drainpipe—drip drip drip, right inta the barrel.

That's leegal, baby, jes drippin along right down the pipe. Bang on the pipe an ask the wrong queshuns an you's *ill*egal, an like as not they gonna find some law t'toss you in jail. But, long's you drippin along deaf t'your own inside mind, you's aye-okay.

You's even allowed t'work up a little steam once in awhile—long's you let it out *lee*gal! In them big noisy words like commonism and capalism. Yeah, you can work up all the mothahfuggin big word steam you wanna, long's you puffin out the ofay noise, ghosty white, cause that's *lee*gal.

An this mothah call the way I'm livin illeegal!

Well baby, I don't say nothin out loud, but inside I give a great big *Hoo-ray!* Hooray for me—long's he don't find out *where* I'm livin illeegal *at!*

An right here is when I know fuggin right well we can't take that dead bored head out t'the I double A double P, an I was outa my dum cottinpickin burrhead t'even *say* it! Gee-zuz, this mothah'd blow the whistle on that place so quick we wouldn't even get time t'pack!

Illeegal! Kee-ryess!

She-it, it ain't really no diffrent'n the way *he's* livin. Us people lookin out for ourseves same as him an them in-charge people lookin out for themseves.

Only big diffrence *I* can see is, we let in most *any*body an *no*body's boss. But them, they can't do that, cause they's in the boss bizness. Let everbody in on the boss end a things, who the fug'd they be boss over? Gee-zuz, they'd go clean outa bizness.

Then he cuts me off thinkin all this, winds down from his gassin, an he say—like he jes got done suckin a lemon—he say, Jes *what*'re you ob*jeck*shuns t'the free ennerprize system, Kitten?

Here's me, comin offa massa's back forty again, I say, Wha'sat sissim, Bay-bae?

*This* system, the *Amer*ikin system!

Oh, oh yeah, uh hum, like you Decent people, you an the bored head.

An him, he say, That's it—free ennerprize!

I say, Well bay-bae, seem like that free ennerprize sissim real nice—for you white people. Got other people takin care a you grits worries pretty good, huh.

An I say, But what about them other people? I mean like poor people, color people. All them other people you got lookin out for you free ennerprize, huh?

He don't say nothin back, so I carry on, I say, No baby, that free ennerprize ain't for me, that's *your* rackit! Me, I like it fine right where I'm at, the I double A double P.

An he say, No no no Kitten, you don't unnerstand! That's commonism!

Yeah?

Yeah!

I say, Well Lover, you right about *one* thing, I sure don't unnerstand. I mean, when you boss people livin offa other people, that's free ennerprize—right? But when some other people tryin t'get you white devils off they backs, that's commonism—right? I say, Baby I don't unnerstand that *no*how!

Claps his hand a-gin his forehead an give out a big moan, an he say, What's the use? No use tryin t'reason with *you!* You jes too unedjukaded!

Yeah, I spose I am. Spose if I was t'get edjukaded, I'd go all this *ize* an *ism* bullshid, and maybe I could even get so high on all that free ennerprize noise I'd never even *see* somebody else's hungry.

Maybe! Same time, I can't help wondering how *he'd* feel —how he'd really *feel,* if he wasn't so fuggin edjukaded, like.

She-it. Seem t'me, whoever boss over the grits an wanna *stay* boss, got a hot word t'lay on anybody try t'come in on the boss end a things. Yeah, an I bet if you was in Russia— that's where the in-charge guys's all commonisms—an if you didn't like bein under them bosses there, why they'd call you a free ennerprizer.

I mean, I ain't never *been* there, but I got a sneakin hunch.

But, anyhow, I shut up. Never shoulda open my big satch on the I double A double P. Shoulda knowed better.

But Kee-ryess, we was all day jes a-settin in that goddam motel room with nothin else t'do, an it's hard t'jes set there takin his bad eye and keepin your mouth shut.

Shoulda done it the hard way. Got him so hopped up mad, it looks like he's goin off his fuggin rocker.

So I cool it, look away an don't pay him no mind for a time.

An after awhile, he say, You er, eh, um, *like* livin there?

Sure do, baby, I say. I like livin there—*in the country.* Like it cause they's so much color. Lotta diffrent greens an browns, an now an then some yella an red. An you'd be surprise all the things goin on out there—river swellin up, fishes jumpin, waterbugs an butterflies, bright an sassy flowers, all them diffrent creetures makin it t'gether. I say, Oh yeah, I like it fine.

Take his mind off the *ize* an *isms*.

Only other thing I tole the mothah was—long about dinner time he ast me, after he got done puttin in a couple phoney phone calls with a hankey over his mouth. Call the police an ast did anybody report a missin person, an then he call some long distance number, tole somebody t'call the bored head's wife, an then he put in one more call, for Zitch t'go fetch dinner.

Then he lean back on that sofa an he say, Kitten tell me somethin—you ever go out an look for a job?

I say, You *serious?*

*Certainly* he's serious.

So I tell him, yeah baby, I done that lookin for a job bit. Was when me an Mary Lou was so bad off, direckly we got let outa jail. Went down t'this departmin store downtown. Mary Lou seen in the papers how they was lookin for Sales. You know, stand behind a couner an sell stuff, Went up some elevader an inta this place, talk t'some white chick, an she give us some paper an pencils, tell us t'fill 'em out.

Go inta this other room an set down, an Mary Lou starts scratchin away on her paper like mad. But me, Geezuz! I can't write! Can't even read! Only numbers—but I goddam well can read numbers, baby, don't you forget *that.*

Anyhow, what I'm sayin, all I done on my pencil was chew. Chew the fuggin paint right off one end watchin Mary Lou scratchin away there.

Then, like she see's I ain't makin it with my pencil an paper, she say, Aw who needs it. Come on.

An we go back out an drop them papers an pencils off with this white chick, an we split.

Mary Lou—like I was feelin bad cause she quit on counta me, I can't write—but she say Oh no, she say they wasn't gonna *hire* nobody, *really!* Jes puttin us through the bit, fillin out forms. She say, Baby you need *pull* t'get you a job, an we ain't got no pull. All we got—she say—all we got, baby, is color. An that don't get you *this* kinda job.

Then he say, Jay See, he say, Tisk tisk tisk. What a defeatis additude! An he wanna know how I got the job at the Fish Pond.

That's diffrent. She-it, that was so simple, I don't know how t'tell the mothah.

See, what happen is, my boyfriend—or is he my bizness manager?—anyhow, Hap makes up tunes, an some a them tunes Herk writ words on, an me, I sing 'em.

So one day, Hap loads me an his guitar in the Voltswagon an we drive downtown an go t'the Fish Pond—they's havin Audishun. Hap plays an I sing, an the man—Kee-ryess! He's hearin it, oh yeah! With his *eyes*—all over my *body!*

Ends up hirin *me!* Tole Hap he already got all the folk singers he can use an he can't hire no more cause that fad's goin out. Tells me if I can learn t'sing these other songs, them mushy ones, I can make a day-bue, an if my singin goes over an if I work out jawin the johns, I'm on.

An you wanna know what he say—Jay See? Say, Kitten that ain't *really* a *job.*

I try t'duck this time, I say, Well baby, I *know.* It's a *gig.*

No no no! He means it ain't a re*speck*able job.

An then he say, Kitten tell you what, *I'll* get you a job.

Yeah? Like what?

Say, Emptyin wastepaper baskets in the Cord House where I work.

For the coundy?

Sure.

I say, What's this emptyin wastepaper baskets thing, huh?

Simple. All you do all day is walk around t'the offices an empty wastepaper baskets.

*Gee-zuz!*

But anyhow, I say, So what's it pay?

What're you makin now?

Forty a week plus tips.

Okay, I'll see to it you get *fifty* a week!

Plus tips?

An he jes laugh, say, Oh no, no tips. You'd be an honest workin girl, Kitten. You'd earn you salry an that would be *it.* Nothin on the side.

I say, Hey baby, you really serious?

*Course* he's serious.

I say, Well thanks but *no* thanks.

She-it. How m'I gonna live on fifty a week? Kee-ryess, I got the whole gang at the headquarders countin on me for grosseries now.

Fifty a week! Shiverin shitfits, baby, you know what grosseries cost? Time the tax done with that fifty an I got done buyin food and gas an them hunner an one what-nots always come up soon's you got a nickel—Gee-zuz! Baby, I'd end up fifty in the fuggin *hole!*

Go round on that awhile, an then dinner comes an we eat.

Three dinners.

An now it's dark out, so we get set t'take off.

But we still ain't sure where the hell we's goin.

Jay See say, We can't go out there, that place you live. No, cause as of *now*, only *two* people know about this, Kitten—you an me. We go there, all those *others*'ll find out.

I feel like sayin you fuggin-aye-right we can't go—*we* can't go there, messinger.

But I keep my big mouth shut, for a change.

I think a minit, an then I come up with this, Say, Hey I got it! Let's take the mothah out t'the quarry, drop him in the water.

Quarry? What quarry?

So I tell him about this place—was an ole stone quarry an now it's a big lake. Put this dead distingwish in his car an run it in—fifty feet deep—an direckly skoopa divers'll find him. Dive down there all the time.

He say, *Yeah*, that's *it*. Say, You know how t'get there?

Sure. Hit the thruway an I'll have us there like right now. Nothin to it.

Say, Come on Kitten, let's put this corps in the Cadillack an go! Come on!

An he's hoppin around havin hiseff a celebrashun.

I get up, an then I think a somethin else. Uh oh. I say, Hold it baby, hold it, you know somethin? Puttin this dead bored head in that car ain't gonna be no easy thing!

We can do it, we can do it, come on! Grabs my hand an pulls me along, say, *Whoopeeee!*

Minit later, there ain't no whoopee, cause we's gruntin again, strainin an sweatin an fartin that chair fulla dead bored head right out the door an tryin t'make it without gettin caught.

Push that chair along bit by bit, up t'the door a the Cadillack.

Jimmy's in a terrible sweat. Scared somebody gonna see us.

Boy, what a sight that would be, huh.

Anyhow, we make it. Kee-ryess, about haff way there I was sure we never gonna do it, cause gettin that distingwish two ton outa that chair an set up for his ride—that was no small thing.

*Whew!* His face turn purple an I saw stars.

Anyhow, we finally get him there, set up in the right-hand side a the front seat, an here goes the bored head, all prim an proper an ready t'go ridin.

Then he turn on me an he say, Can, eh . . . can, eh . . . can you *drive*, Kitten?

*Sure* I can drive!

Say, You, eh . . . got a lyssins?

Oh hell no, but I can *drive*, don't you worry over that. Come on, let's go.

Rolls his eyes, an he say, Okay, let's go.

Flips me the keys t'the Thunderbird an goes around an climbs in the Cadillack.

Dam near looks alive, that distingwish gentlemin, settin there in that front seat. Put his hat on his head an pull it down in front some, looks like he's jes settin there snoozin.

Till you get up close an see his eyes.

Mr. Pennypacker, rest his soul, was thereafter found to be missing. That Sunday, in fact, I received a phone call from Axelrod Stuffert, Chief of the County Police, and Al wanted to know if I knew where the board head was.

Well, I had just returned from church when his call came in, and I remember thinking it curious that the Chairman hadn't attended that Sunday. He was a regular at church.

"Al," I said with penetrating concern, "what do you mean?"

"He's missing," said the Chief. "Been missing since Friday, and you were the last one to be seen with him."

Now at this important juncture, I should have told the *whole* story—especially to Al, who is in solid with the majority faction and so wouldn't breathe a word of the Chairman's little Friday night diversion, but instead would simply conduct a free and open investigation into the really meaningful facts. However, at the time, I hadn't the faintest idea that the board head was not only dead, but that the whole thing would eventually be pitched and tossed on the dangerous seas of conjecture.

But I'm sure you can well understand how, at *that* time, my uppermost concern was to protect Mr. Pennypacker's good name. Which is why I replied to Al as follows:

"The last time I saw him, Al, was when he left the Fish Pond. We went out to dinner at Blattenfeld's, and later we went on to the Fish Pond for a couple of drinks, and then—oh, about midnight, I guess it was—the Chairman left for home."

Which, as you know, Dear Reader, wasn't exactly the whole story in its entirety. In all honest truth, I should have been more co-operative with Al, and the only reason I wasn't was, as I've mentioned, that I didn't know, at the time, that Mr. Pennypacker had *not* gone straight home. From the motel.

However, he was thereafter among the missing. For a week and a half, and it wasn't until a couple of scuba divers went bounty hunting in some old abandoned stone quarry on the northern border of our County that he was found—that his *body* was found—fifty feet down in the cold waters of this old quarry, in his Cadillac.

For the week and a half preceding this discovery, the search for him had been frantic, and nation-wide. You'll probably recall hearing of it, if you think about it a moment, for it was thoroughly covered—all the big networks zeroed in on the facts of his mysterious disappearance.

My nerves, during that week and a half of national network attention, were in a frightful state, as I'm sure you can well imagine. In addition to which, it became my distasteful task to gather and compile biographical material about the illustrious Chairman, just in case.

And if I live to be a hundred, I won't forget the day his body was found. It was a Wednesday, and we learned about it at lunch. The board meets each Monday and Wednesday morning, and we had just adjourned to that restaurant across the street from the Courthouse, and we had—at the moment Benny burst in with the news—just ordered a round of drinks. Which never came, of course, for we were off like flashes for the scene as soon as Benny (Benjamin Toutman, a very heads-up reporter) told us the news—that entire board and all associated personnel, twenty-five people in all.

For he had been found, Dear Reader, by scuba divers, as mentioned, in this old quarry that abuts the east side of Legislative Route 22405, a little-traveled gravel affair running from the Governor Glassfort Thruway to the quarry.

We drove there, that fateful Wednesday, in a convoy of five cars, with my Thunderbird containing four others besides myself, and bringing up the rear. We arrived on the scene to find a large crane had just lifted the illustrious board head's Cadillac from the depths of those murky waters.

The Chairman himself was in a state of—his *body* was in the process of decomposition. It was awful!

But—to pass over these lurid details—a search of the entire surrounding area was made by our very diligent police force. And even though they found not a single clue, *that* wasn't *their* fault, for they searched long and hard, for days and days!

Well, the air has been simply full of rumors ever since. One story has it that the Chairman went to Senator Schlitzer's home that Friday and stayed the night. Which rumor has a starting point in reality, as you'll recall my showing you. That is, it came about as a direct result of that telephone call I made at the request of the ailing Mr. Pennypacker—a well-intentioned attempt to protect his wife from worry. It's just unfortunate that this well-intentioned attempt should have resulted in these nasty rumors, for the Senator has been pelted with questions ever since.

But another story has it that I *enticed* the board head into a wild night of drunken debauchery, which precipitated a heart attack, which killed him, and that he was thereafter *thrown* into the quarry—no doubt by whatever underworld characters *I* brought him into contact with—as this story would have it—thrown into the quarry by *them!*

But over and above all these wild, outlandish, unsubstantiated figments of the sick imaginations of malicious gossips, there is this dilemma: our County authorities, to this day, are completely at a loss, for they are naturally reluctant to declare the eminent man's demise a *suicide,* but on the other hand, can find no evidence to support any other theory.

And my account, I fear, will shed no light on this. There still remains the mystery of what happened to him after

Abel Zitch and I saw him leave the motel in his car on his way home.

I blame myself. I should have followed him all the way home. Better yet, I should have driven him myself.

However, that's a useless sentiment. There are things in every man's life that, if he had it to do over again, would be done differently. Aren't there?

At any rate, one thing is certain—and has now been officially established, as of the writing of this account of the actual facts, and that is this: that it's quite obvious that I had nothing to do with Mr. Pennypacker's tragic demise, and as far as that one pointedly malicious rumor is concerned, I did—yes—introduce him to a colored whore, Kitten, who was—yes—a one-time acquaintance of mine, and also underworld. But—repeat but—this introduction came about at *his* request, not mine.

And it was—true—probably this perverse attraction for Kitten which he was feeling that fateful Friday which proved too much for his valiant heart. If I hadn't let myself be persuaded by him to make this introduction and take that motel room and escort her out there to him, he might have gone straight home from the Fish Pond, retired to bed and not overtaxed his ailing organ.

Hindsight, however, will get us nowhere. The fact remains that I did act on his behalf, and that tragedy did result. My friends all tell me not to blame myself for this, that they would have done the same in my place, but one can't help harboring regrets, deep regrets.

And while I'm on the subject of regrets, I might as well mention that I also regret my shortcomings as a creative artist: namely, I desperately wish I could recreate the eminent board head so he would *live* for you. I fear that if you weren't privileged to have met the man himself, in the flesh, my shortcomings might leave you with the impression that he was the flimsy figment of some fiction writer's fractured imagination. Which is probably because, in certain respects, he was—actually—bigger than life.

Especially his speeches. Mr. Pennypacker, rest his soul, will always be remembered here for his oratory, for he wasn't one of your philosophical New Frontiersmen, bent over by the weight of a Phi Beta Kappa key on his gizzard. He spoke plain and he made sense—good sound economical sense—and he made it loud and clear. We used to joke about how, when he rendered a moving ovation in the board's hearing room, the whole Courthouse sounded like feeding time in the lions cage at the zoo.

And although Hook County is not without its champions of free enterprise—nor, with God on our side, will we ever be—there seems to be none who can adequately replace Mr. P. as the virile and forceful spearhead that he was, especially when it comes to dealing with such as the aforementioned lace-pantie lunacy out of Welfare.

Which, I might say right here, was dealt with. My report was read by Herskovitz, in the Chairman's absence, who followed this reading by an eloquent speech about how charity can never be a substitute for Social Justice, and besides, the poor of *our* County don't *want* give-away hand-outs and government subsidies—they value their independence too much for *that!* It was a speech of apocalyptic brilliance, and a fitting footnote to my report. The vote being 5–3 against the motion to allocate this $3,000. Motion made by Goodfellow, of course. And it was

George Washington Jones, the first Negro member of our board in over a century, who cast the deciding vote. He saw the light at the last minute and went with the majority faction—a smart move on the part of this extraordinary newcomer, who is not only a credit to his race, but gives our board a fine image, holding us aloof from charges of racial prejudice.

Yet, somehow, with the Chairman's demise, something clean and good about the spirit of our efforts against welfarism is missing. Strange how one man of exceptionally large stature can be such a heavy influence in these matters, isn't it.

And the power vacuum which now exists in Hook County is simply awesome; the jockeying for political control grows daily more vicious. For instance, it's been stoutly rumored that Humphrey Goodfellow has, in public, called my function the—quote public relations racket unquote—and declared *me* a *political hack!*

Deeply shaken as I am by such disrespect for the dead—because by now, he knows perfectly well that Mr. Pennypacker was, finally, in the end, totally in favor of me and my function—I am not at all incapable of coping with Hump. By groundwork laid in other areas, I'm far from whipped by *his* intimidations, and if instead of working for the common good of us all, he decides to play it rough, I'll be ready for him. Because, you see, Mr. Goodfellow, wild-eyed liberal that he is, has had an affair—with *my secretary!* Yes, Betty Lu! Who, I can't resist mentioning, keeps a tape recorder under her bed. And I should know, because it was none other than J. C. Holland who purchased that tape recorder. As a present to her. How she uses it, or where she keeps it, is *her* business.

And . . . well, there just doesn't seem much more I can say, for I believe I've covered my ground quite thoroughly. And without resorting to sex or violence, both of which have been so tediously overdone in our literature of late.

So there just isn't anything left to add, I suppose.

Oh! Except, per chance, for that funeral! Yes, I should mention that funeral, for it was certainly a ceremony to purify the heart—a momentous occasion, and there's been nothing quite like it before or since.

Every flower shop in the County hummed with business as that funeral approached, preparing hundreds of baskets and wreaths, each striving to out-display the others, and the Gray Memorial Home on Cherry Street literally overflowed with flowers, bright and sweet-smelling, which became so numerous, eventually, that the Gray management was forced to fill both its business and personal garages, removing three hearses and all family cars to make way for flowers. And still more came—from all over the County, from the State Capitol, from the departed man's admirers in Washington—why, we even received a telegram from the President himself! Sent, of course, by his public relations people!

Yes, it was an outpouring of appreciation for a demised public official unequaled in all Hook history, those flowers, telegrams, telephone calls, and not excluding the television coverage, which focused the attention of the entire nation on this most momentous event, a fitting finale to the running account TV did on his mysterious disappearance.

And the service itself was no less horrendous—a gathering of such magnitude that only a detailed listing of who's who in Hook County could do it justice. Everyone, it seemed, came! So many, in fact, that a system of priorities had to be established to decide who would be permitted inside the funeral home for the service, and then whose car would be at what point in the long procession to Green Haven Memorial Park—a procession which moved with such proud dignity down Center Avenue that it imbued the entire city with a hush of reverence for the departed Chairman, casting a hallowed pall of shadow and sorrow, loss and perplexity over all who saw it from the sidewalks, and even, it seemed, dimming for a moment the colorful façade of our prosperous business district. For it was a line of cars so long that it stopped cross-Center traffic for over an hour.

Then, at Memorial Park, only a handful of those paying their final respects could be grave-side on the special bleachers hastily erected—with the Senator and I front and center flanking the bereaved widow—while hundreds lined the spiked iron fence surrounding the park, eager to be present for this last moment of tribute before the great man's casket was lowered into his final resting place and his soul arose to its eternal repose.

He's drivin the bored head's Cadillack, an I'm drivin the Thunderbird.

Follow him outa the motel, then I take the lead an he tails the Bird. Go t'the thruway an take that, cut off on this gravel road out near where the I double A double P's at.

Make it t'the quarry, an I park the Bird back near the bushes where Hap always parks the Voltswagon when he takes everbody swimmin. Jay See pulls up along side—*mmmmmm*, rolls down the lecktrick winda an he say, This it?

Yeah but we gotta make sure nobody's here, that's the first thing.

Full moon out again t'night—so big an bright it makes our shadows—an if somebody around here anyplace, they gonna see us plain's day, so I tell him, scout the place, take a walk around.

He don't like that idea, but he takes his trip anyhow. Road goes part way around, an then you take a path.

Comes back an I say, Okay ofay, hop in that Cad an ease him right up that rock there, right t'the edge, an keep the fuggin lights out, you hear?

Like, they got this high rock here, that's what Hap an them dive offa, an you can drive a car right up an off this rock, too. Fifty feet deep down unner that rock, an this Cad ain't gonna be the first car they fished outa here neither. She-it. Baby, there for a time, Herk was unloadin bout one hot set a wheels a week offa this rock.

Gets the Cadillack driv up there by the light a the moon, an I come strollin along behind, puttin on real bossy. Get there, an he's settin with the engine idelin.

I say, Okay now what we gotta do is, we gotta find a big stone, big enough so we can set it on the gas peddle an keep the engine runnin. You hip? So okay, hop out, messinger, an suck up a stone. An make sure it's a flat one, too, cause they's the best for settin on gas peddles. Won't roll off.

Gets out lookin, walks back down the high rock huntin. Comes back, got hiseff a pretty good one. Flat, heavy, big enough.

Then he stands there a minit lookin at me, like waitin for more orders. Already tole him that goddam stone goes on the gas, but it didn't sink in. So I tell him again, say, Okay now you put the stone on the gas.

Dum she-it.

Takes awhile for him t'make up his mind t'do this. Stands there lookin in the Cadillack at his dead friend, holdin that stone.

I say, Baby there ain't no use you sayin goodbye t'you distingwish gentlemin cause he ain't *there* no more t'hear it. Come on, put the stone on.

Gets the stone set down okay. Engine's runnin fast now —*vroomm!* Top speed. An then he pops back outa that Cad like he's scared it's gonna take off with him in it.

I say, Hey baby, don't run away yet. You still got one more step. One moe. C'mere Lover, one moe time.

That's what I tell *him.* Me, I'm keepin plenty a room tween me an that screamin Cadillack, you bet you sweet life! Cause when he puts that thing in gear—look out! Lotta little stones around here, an when them wheels start spinnin, you jes never know how them stones gonna fly. An you ain't even sure the ass end a that car won't whip around an put it goin in the wrong direckshun. Kee-ryess, I seen one car spin around on Herk an take him in that quarry with it, slant-wise. So me, I'm standin back.

An I'm tellin the dum mothah what he gotta do—go over an put that fuggin thing in gear an jump back quick, outa the way. I say, Now baby, one thing you gotta make sure of—don't put that thing in *reverse!*

Nods his head.

Another thing—I say—you gotta reach in an flip that thing in gear, an then, baby, you gotta get you arm back outa there—*quick*. You hear? Get you arm out an youseff away, fast's you can.

Nods again.

Then he goes sneakin up on that thing on the driver's side—bored head jes a-settin there nice's can be, waitin for his flyin ride. Reaches in an puts that thing in gear, an then he makes a jump back like I never even seen Herk make. I mean, he musta left the ground six feet down on his way back outa there—up in the air, hits the ground an does a roll.

Well I don't blame him none for that. Cause it don't take long for that gear t'catch ahold an that car t'take off. An this one's a good clean job, too. Wheels catch, an up up an away she goes.

Good-bye-eee-eee bored head!

Nice's can be, that Cad jes goes right up with that dead bored head drivin from the righthand side, an over she goes, off inta mid-air an down.

KERR FLOOM! Splash goes way up t'the sky.

Me an Jimmy run up t'the edge an look down—splash dies down, an there's the water, bubblin an boilin an cookin up a big shot politicko, bubble bubble bubble.

Then he say, Well that's that.

I say, Check man, the end!

But I sed that end bit too fuggin soon. Yeah, cause that was like hell the end. Oh no. This sumbitch, he got some other end in mind. Yeah, he got one moe time in mind.

Here's how that one goes.

He say, Well . . . Kitten if you see me around the Fish Pond or the City, don't let on you know me.

Don't worry, I won't.

But all the time he's givin me this talk an himmin an hawin around like that, my meddle telepathy's goin wild over somethin. Cause, like, I can hear his brains rattlin, can hear turnin goin on in that skull a his, loud's the Cadillack engine, an I know somethin's comin—but I don't know what!

Now what I shoulda done is, I shoulda left, right now! Jes walked off that rock an set myseff down in that Bird, wait for him t'drop me off near home.

She-it. Gee-zuz, baby! What I really shoulda done is run back down an driv that Bird home myseff! Left the bastid. Yeah, that's what I shoulda done.

Anyhow, what I'm sayin, I didn't do nothin. Jes stood there lissenin t'him puttin on that sad talk, tryin t'tune in on that noise in his skull.

Kitten, I sure hate t'say good-bye like this. Kitten, I want you t'know somethin . . .

More himmin an hawin, don't really say nothin for sure, but I got the drift—he's tellin me how much he likes me.

My ass! My ass's what he likes, cause he can't see me for my sex an skin. Only that ain't what he *say*in he likes. Sayin he likes *me!*

What he's leadin up to—he moves in an puts his arms around me. Nice an easy, this time.

She-it, I'da been longgone, he'da come on rough. Top a this rock ain't no place t'get rough. But he's comin on sweet an good, so I let this action go awhile. I say t'myseff, Well baby, you got a hunner outa this mothah an peenuts outa the distingwish. Tole you you was gonna make at least a hunner—at least—an that least is all you made, really. Cause you can't count that peenuts.

Oh, I forgot t'tell that part—while we was pullin on that fat cat's pants back in the motel I slip a hand in his pocket an come up with a moneyclip, right unner Jay See's nose. Only trouble, later on I look an all that sumbitch's carryin on him was seven dollahs! That's all, seven ones.

Anyhow, what I'm sayin, if this Jimmy boy wants him one moe quickie, an if he got one moe fifty, I might jes's well put that jingle in my churchbell—right? Might's well be in *my* bell, cause *he* sure don't need it. He's ringin up more fifties all the time!

So I let him play around. Then when I figure he's up good an ready, I say, *Gee* Lover, I don't wanna sound *mean*, but *Gee* Sweetheart, I can't *make* it with you—right *here*, I mean, right *now!* I mean, for less than *fifty!*

Don't say a word back on that. Reaches around an goes down inside my leatards an unnerneath my pants, starts playin in there.

I make noises like I'm enjoyin it, then I say, Ooh-wee, I wish I could, baby, but I jes can't. You gotta unnerstand. Please try t'unnerstand. I say, Fifty—but not—one cent more!

Maybe it was that little touch a nastiness, I don't know. But nex thing I know, this motherin messinger's comin on real rough with me. Tryin t'unzip my leatards and get straight at my bizness.

I start squirmin, tryin t'stay loose. Say, Fifty dollahs, Lover, an you can take you choice. Lay fifty on me, baby, use me any way you wanna.

An when he don't say nothin back on *that,* I start really movin, tryin t'get away. Start tellin him t'forget it, fug off, let's leave. But he ain't for leavin. No, he's for right now, on top a this rock, tryin t'get me, free.

An here we go, big scene. I'm wormin around tryin t'get loose, an he's hangin on, workin me over with boff hands. An pretty soon I'm puttin up a squawk, an if I'da knowed somebody was around, baby, I'da been puttin up a holler. Way it was, I'm fightin the mothah, tryin t'get free. Yeah, he's tryin t'get *me* free, an I'm tryin t'*get* free!

Well baby, the nex thing I know, I'm in mid-air! Yeah! Oh yeah! One minit I'm dancin around on top a that rock with Jay See, an the nex minit I'm in mid-fuggin-air!

Fallin, baby, what I'm doin now. Fallin fallin fallin. Right off the end a that goddam rock!

An about all I can recall is sayin t'myseff, Okay Girl, this is *it!* Skoopa divers gonna find one color girl down here when they fish that dead distingwish out. Yeah! Cause —I can't swim!

Gee-zuz, I tried it, baby, I tried swimmin, but I sink like a rock. Hap was gonna teech me, but it didn't do no good. Sink ever time.

So here goes me—*down.* Good fuggin night, happy landin, the end. An when I hit that water—*ooh wee!* You should see how dark that is. An the more down I go, the darker it gets. An baby, I mean t'tell ya, I'm goin *down,* too. Goin down like I'm sure I'm never gonna *stop* goin down.

Ain't so dum about swimmin I try t'breathe that water. No, I been unner water before, been through that bit. So I hold my stupid breath. Yeah! Only smart thing I done all night, hold my breath.

Down down down, holdin all the everlovin air I got in

me when I hit that water. Forgot all about that pocketbook, but she-it. I don't have no worry there—my fingers around the strap a that thing good an tight, an they know t'hang on. That's somethin they *know*, baby, I don't gotta tell 'em.

Then—like before I even got up from down straight—here goes me, I'm up. Yeah, right up on top a the water. Went down an come up. Don't know how the fug I ever made it back up, but here I am.

Move, Girl, move! Got my arms goin like windmills an my legs runnin in that water fast's I can make 'em go. An guess what. Down again. That's me, down unner again I go.

Gee-eee-eee-zuz! Then, like I been holdin my breath all this time—right? Okay, I run out. Can't hold it no longer. I try, but my lungs jes plain give up, go right ahead on they own an take a breath, only—steada air, they get water. Sticks in my throat, liked t'gag me t'death, liked t'pop the top a my head right off.

Well baby, I'm still in there tryin—everthin goin fast's they can go, arms an legs. I mean you ain't puttin this girl down if she can help it. Long's she got one last move, she gonna make it. So I'm movin. Don't know which direckshun I'm goin, but I'm movin. Flyin in that water like a pee-petrified-fuggin-duck in pee soup.

Recall thinkin they was rocks around here some place. I seen them rocks from the top a the big rock t'night, an they's what Hap an June an them use. Dive in, swim over, grab ahold. You can get out on them rocks, an then they's this path, takes you right around the bottom of the big rock an up t'the top again.

An what happen is, I feel my purse hit somethin an I guess that musta been a rock. Reach over in that direck-shun, an I—baby, I *claw* my way in that water, an sure enough, it's a rock.

How I find out is, I hit the fuggin thing with my head. Gee-zuz! Gotta get hit over the head with it, fore I know it's here.

Anyhow, grab that rock, an boy do I come outa that water. Like a moon-goin monkey. But that's about's far as I make it. I mean, I fall right down an take a coughin fit, tryin t'get that water outa my throat an lungs. Feels like I got a basin stopper in that throat.

Then, KERR FLOOM! Great big splash goes up right behind me. Say t'myseff, Don't pay no mind t'that, Girl, it's jes some asstranot fallin outa the sky.

She-it, I don't even look around t'see what it is. Jes hear this big splash an keep right on with my coughin fit.

Really, baby, I'll tell ya—what I really thought was, it must be Jay See, divin in for his free piece. An I bet that's who you think it was, too, huh.

Wrong!

Cause, nex thing, somebody pushin me down on the rock an breathin inta my mouth.

That's when I know who it is—Hap, cause I can taste the mothah.

Got air goin in an out now. Heart's hoppin around in there like he's gonna jump clear out any minit, but I'm with it again. An I say—here's me, like this—I say, Where . . . you . . . come . . . from?

Hap say he was hidin right near by in the brush, been

hangin on all day. Follow us out here, drive along behind with his lights out. Went by moonlight.

Then he say, Looks like I come jes in time, huh, Couzin. Like in the movies, Ra-da-da-Dot-da-Dah! Cavalry come in the nick a time.

Me, I say, Like hell! You . . . was . . . *late!*

An after I catch my breath, I tell the sumbitch, cause he's talkin like he pulled me out! So I put him straight, let him know I ain't fallin for that ole cornball con.

Say, Hey Couzin, you was *late!* Get that through you cornpone skull. I was already *on* that rock when *you* come in.

An all he can say is, Well Couzin, I give it a good try, you gotta admit. Then he say, Lissen, I want you t'know somethin. White man push you in—right? An a white man try, he *tried* t'pull you *out.*

Thinks Jay See push me in. Don't matter what I say, he thinks Jay See push me in. That's what he *wanna* think, cause then he can pull a one-up on me.

But I ain't got no mind for that noise right now. Lookin around, don't see that messinger nowhere in sight. Lookin all around, wonderin where in the hell he got to. Him an that Thunderbird gone like they never was here.

Not a sign of em. Gee-zuz!

Walkin back t'the Voltswagon, my head's on a swivel, huntin. Got that car parked down the road in a clump a trees. He's jabberin an I'm lookin, an finally I say, Hey Couzin, come off you burden kick a minit an tell me somethin—where'd that john go? What the fug happen t'that Thunderbird?

Hap say, Oh he musta took off in a big cloud a dust.

Was on top a the rock takin off his clothes, but I zoom right by an dove right in, clothes an all, so I guess he jes took off.

How bout that!

Didn't even stop t'say good-bye.

I bet Hap musta scare the bee-gee-zes outa him, huh. Comin outa nowhere like that.

Then Hap's right back on his confederit bit—all the way home he's yakkin away—Gettin so you niggers can't tell a white man from a white man! Ring some a that water outa you brain, Girl.

I'm lippin off right back, but he jes keeps it up—That goddam Abraham Liggin's the one started all the fuggin trouble, forefather's was makin good time, turnin you black Africans the prettiest shade a brown an that goddam Liggin come along, hand all you color couzins over t'them goddam yankee capalist pigs, rewrite histry, starve you, put you down so far it cut the ground right out from unner my family tree.

Piss on that family tree! What I tell that mothahfuggah once I get it up t'here with all this ole deckadent depose southern aristockrsy noise he's always puttin out. An if I'da had an ounce a pep left in me, there'd a been a race riot in that Voltswagon before we got back t'the headquarders.

I mean me an Hap always jokin around about how he's carryin the white man's burden, cause he's the offspring a ole deckadent depose southern aristockrsy, an that's why he call me Couzin an all—but Kee-ryess! Enough's ee-fuggin-*nuff!* An if I'da had more pep, he'd a got that water-logged pocketbook right over top a his deckadent depose blond-headed noggin!

Was about all I could manage, way things was, t'tell him if he don't shut the hell up on that bullshid right this minit, I'm gonna take off an join the Black Muslims an be right with 'em when we go back t'Dixie an roast them white biggits in canable pots, eat one a day for dinner.

Was a pretty loud ride in that Voltswagon, all the way back t'the headquarders, an only one good thing come out of it—Hap forgot his main queshun. Forgot t'ast about the money. Clean forgot all the way home!

Didn't think a thing about it till we was pullin in through the gate, an then—like, by this time I got him pretty quiet, cause I been puttin up the biggest yakkin, last couple miles —an goin in the gate, he say, Well Couzin, besides pushin you in the water, did that ofay bastid ever *pay?*

I can't get him off sayin Jay See *push* me in, so I jes let him go right on thinkin that. Gonna think it anyhow. But on the money, I'm jes in the right mood t'give him a bad time. Yeah! So this time, baby, I put the clamps down.

I say, Gee Hap, you know what happen? He put fifty in my hand back in the club, an then, out in the motel, he took it *back!*

An Hap, the dum she-it, he be*lieves* it! Ha! Don't even dip inta my bra, forgets all about that.

An then, direckly we walk inta the headquarders, everbody come buzzin around—an here's us, ringin wet an makin puddles, Hap's shoes squeekin an squishin.

He's walkin back an forth, squish-squashin an tellin everbody what happen—*his* story on it. An me, I take off upstairs an get outa my wet things. Empty out that pocketbook, clean it out best I can, an then I hop unner a nice warm shower.

Pretty soon, Hap climb in with me—everbody still hangin in, lissenin t'what he's tellin 'em. They stand there watchin us shower an wash each other's backs, an he's still swingin on his story the whole time.

She-it, he put more *in* than I ever knowed was *there*, that story.

Then I get dress quick's I can, do my hair in a hurry, best I can in such a big rush, an I set up a holler for him t'make it snappy or I'll be late for the club—an *then* what's everbody gonna do, huh? Cause t'night's payday!

But, drivin back t'the city, I set him straight. Gee-zuz, I get tired lissenin t'all his noise, so I reach down inta my pocketbook—had t'take 'em outa my wet bra—an I haul up them bills. Shove 'em at him, tell him t'take the money an shut up. Don't run, jes shut up.

So! That's about the sum cottinpickin total.

That money put us eatin good again. Mary Lou an Perry went bustin they ass buyin grosseries.

I had a bad time tryin t'tell the man at the club what happen t'his dress, but Sharmain back me up, tole him Jay See got her drunk one night an put her unner a shower, clothes an all. So that's jes what I tole the man he done t'me, too, an once I got that story over, it was okay.

Got a new dress, an you should see them flush johns I'm fishin outa that Fish Pond lounge now. Ain't goin in there after 'em no more, neither.

Was over the radio an on tee vee an all about the bored head being missin, an there for a time I was afraid nobody went skoopa divin no more. But they found the mothah, finally, about a week an a haff later.

An then, the nex Saterday, they put on this big funeril.

Me an Hap drove in for that. Couldn't rezist goin. Watch it all from the outside a this iron fence they got goin round the semetary.

Not much you can see. Jes a big mob scene, everbody all done up in gladrags, comin on real big an sad. In this jam-up around where they put this very distingwish gentlemin back in the ground.